The Templar Curse

CW01019913

Phillip Ross

ISBN:1517027284
ISBN-13:9781517027285

DEDICATION

For Dad
4th July 1940 - 6th July 2103

Foreword

Before we begin our story I would like to tell you a little about the characters and events depicted in this story, Many of whom are based on actual historical figures and events from out rich history.

William Lyvett and his Templar Companions were actual Knights Templar from the Yorkshire Preceptories their lives may have played out differently to the story I have included them in and I hope if any of their descendants are alive that they are in no way offended by my use of their names.

I must also extend this to the Scottish ancestors of Robert The Bruce and the other Scottish Lairds mentioned.

Although much of the events of this story are based on fact the story of the Templar Treasure will always remain a mystery and this is purely a fictional story.

Phillip Ross.

CONTENTS

ACKNOWLEDGMENTS

Big thank you to Alan Hall for proof reading the book and with his help in researching.

Prologue:

In the year 1118 AD, a French family of noble birth set forth to ride to the holy lands.

Hugh De Payens and Eight of his close relatives began the order of the Knights Templar to protect Pilgrims on their journey to the holy land.

By the 13th Century the Templar order had become large in numbers and had now set up Preceptories across the known world.

These Preceptories were farmsteads growing crops and breeding cattle, they were also the centre for a profitable venture.

The Knights were sworn to poverty themselves yet they set up a banking system. A Pilgrim would leave their valuables and gold in return for a Chit, a small piece of paper with the amount deposited written on it.

It would be signed by the head Preceptor to be cashed in on the Pilgrim's arrival in the holy land.

The Templar Knights had fought in all the eight Crusades and now as the ninth ended many Knights made their way home to Europe and a dream of peace.

Phillip Ross

1 THE TEMPLAR'S JOURNEY

The night was as thick as velvet shrouding a golden blanket, each thread crumbled beneath weary feet. Two figures stumbled across the sand, the bitter cold of the Arabian night stinging at the exposed parts of their bodies and faces. A swift wind drove dust into their eyes, yet after all the bloodshed they had seen, to endure this torment was bliss in comparison.

Ahead of the figures loomed a small structure, unseen in the blizzard they almost collided with the walls. " look we have found shelter my friend" shouted one of the figures as they clambered through the doorway and into the solitude of the hut. Here they would rest safe from the sand storm and cold until the morning, it would be then the heat and sand would torment them once more.

A small fire in the centre of the hovel crackled as it's flames leapt toward the ceiling. Two men huddled around it's pitiful flame relishing the little heat it provided. The man whom had spoken placed a battered steel helm beside him on the floor and let out a sigh as he ran his fingers over a deep dent in the crown of the armoured head piece. "you should have thrown that helm after that heathen crushed your head" laughed his companion.

The first man glanced up and smiled "I keep it as a reminder that none of us are immortal, if it was not for this helm and my armour I would not be here to say these words and breathe in that awful stench that is protruding from you". He smiled and turned back to the fire staring longingly into the flames.

The owner of the helm was not a young man, yet his forty five years had treated him kindly and apart from a thin grey streak in his long beard he had a full head of dark brown hair flowing freely over his shoulders. His eyes were kind and gentle yet held visions of horror seen through many years and many a battle, the scar down his right cheek was a war trophy given to him by a Saracen five years earlier.

He wore the tunic of the Order of The Knights Templar, as did his companion who lay with his back to the wall chewing stale bread he had found in a small cupboard. He offered the remainder to his friend "here William it will help keep your strength up" he said letting the bread drop into William's lap.

William Lyvett the IV picked up the bread and ate, trying his hardest to keep the foul tasting food in his stomach he brushed the crumbs from his tunic. "Thank you Geoffrey, let us rest and when we wake in the morning we head for the coast, then across the sea to home".

He wanted to believe they would make it to England's shore as much as Geoffrey Jolif did.

The Two men had been neighbours before they joined the Crusades, their Preceptories being only a few miles apart.

The fire began to die down and the two knights settled into a deep sleep, they were haunted by dreams of diabolical deeds, all done in the name of God.

The hours passed and William awoke, he checked the lining of his tunic, breathing a sigh of relief he felt the soft bulge of the envelope he had been given by the

Grand Master. Only he knew of its whereabouts and none but the Grand Master himself knew the contents.

All William knew was that he was to deliver the letter to the Preceptor at Copmanthorpe.

The air was still, chilly yet not bitter and morning was close, William lent over, picked up his sword and prodded his companion in the thigh. "Geoffrey wake up we must go before the sun rises and becomes scalding" he said standing up and gathering his belongings.

Geoffrey stirred and followed suit, soon the hovel was out of sight and the two men were once more trundling over the desert dunes.

The desert was eventually broken by a vast region of grey mountains, vegetation grew in scattered patterns between the boulders which were now unwanted obstacles to the two Templar. This area was still hostile to Christians and any that were found wandering the mountains were usually tortured and sold into slavery, a fate that both William and Geoffrey wished to avoid.

Days and nights turned into weeks, weeks into months and soon supplies were running low but an abundance of wild fruit, found as they descended the mountainous terrain, soon filled their empty bellies.

As they ate the sweet juicy grapes and apples they heard voices approaching the orchard, silently they slid behind a large fallen birch out of sight.

A group of four men and a young woman all carrying baskets walked toward the apple trees and began to pick the ripe fruit from the branches, filling their baskets. The young woman dropped a large apple which rolled toward the fallen birch tree, she swore in a language William did not recognise and began to clamber over the trunk, she slipped and fell, landing face first between William and Geoffrey as she picked herself up she felt hands grasp her and pull her back to the ground, a large gauntlet covered her mouth muffling her shriek for help.

"Silence" whispered William pinning the woman to the muddy floor, he peered over the trunk and saw the men walking further into the orchard, they didn't seem to notice their female companion had disappeared.

William slowly removed his hand from the woman's mouth "scream and I shall cut your throat" he said slipping the blade of his dagger beneath the woman's chin. The woman didn't speak, she sobbed softly, tears ran down her dirt covered cheeks leaving tracks on her face, she rubbed her eyes with a grubby hand and glared at William with a look of one who had known pain.

He looked the woman up and down, drinking in the faded beauty beneath the unwashed mask, dark brown eyes stared back at him, her hair was matted and stuck to her face like tar, he couldn't help but smile.

William straightened his lips and spoke " what is your name?" he asked, the woman didn't reply she just stared defiantly into his deep blue eyes, studying his features and determining his purpose.

"What.... is..... your....name?" he asked more slowly this time "Miana, m...my name it is Miana" she stammered softly in broken English "you are Englishman yes?" she asked, William nodded his head "we are knights of the Temple of Solomon making our way home to England" he replied.

Miana smiled "English are friends, no?" she asked, William didn't quite understand the question "what Country is this?" he asked in reply, "Bulgaria" said Miana standing up and dusting herself down "come, we help you" she smiled beckoning for William and Geoffrey to follow.

The smell of freshly brewed apple cider drifted up the Templar's noses "another tankard my Englishman friends" asked one of the four men who had been introduced to William and Geoffrey as Talan. "Thank you for your hospitality Talan" said Geoffrey as he downed the contents of his mug and held it forward to be refilled.

Bellies full and drink flowing the men and Miana settled beside the fire. None had spoken about the wars in the East till now, Johanda a tall gangly man with long blonde hair was the first to mention it. "So tell me what was it like Sir William?" his English was very good, taught to him by a missionary Johanda had excelled at the language and out of his companions he was the most fluent.

William looked into his drink, half expecting to see his reflection shimmer and disappear only to be replaced by images of the past.

This did not happen however and slightly disappointed he lifted his head and began to tell of the horror and blood he had seen during his thirty years in the service of God.

William finished his tale and sat back to finish his drink, a voice from the shadows alerted him " is this why King Philip of France has declared the Templar's outlaws in all countries?" Geoffrey stood up and drew his sword, much to the dismay and alarm of the other occupants "how dare you say such a thing, show yourself sir" he demanded waving his blade at the dark recess.

The figure stood and approached the firelight.

He was an elderly man possibly in his late nineties, he stumbled and was caught by William. Nodding in thanks he sat down beside Miana and Johanda.

William steadied Geoffrey's blade with his hand, lowering it to point toward the ground "be still Geoffrey I am sure the old man meant no harm". Sir Geoffrey grumbled to himself and sat back down, burying himself in his cider.

"So old man pray tell me what you know of our order ?" asked William following suit and placing himself back on the rug. The old man sniffled "only what I hear from my brother in Germany" he reached over and grabbed Geoffrey's tankard which had momentarily been placed on the floor in front of him.

The old man gulped down the contents much to the amusement of his companions and the distaste of Geoffrey, William grinned at the charade, "I received a letter from my brother only yesterday stating that some of your brethren had been rounded up in his village" began the old man.

"It seems the King of France is charging the order with heresy and crimes against God and the church" he coughed and wheezed several times before continuing "my brother says that all Templar are being rounded up and tried". William shook his head "no this can not be, we must get home and speak with the preceptors, thank you old man your words have been very helpful" he turned to the other occupants "We thank you for your hospitality but we must leave for the shore at once".

William felt a hand on his arm and looked down, Miana looked back up at him, her eyes pleading for him to stay, knowing this was impossible, she sighed and stood. "We have horses, please help yourselves to the best ones, let me prepare supplies for your journey" she busied herself placing food and drink into sacks as Talan led them to the stables and helped prepare two shabby looking mares.

"These are our best horses, Medina and salanka they will see you are safe till you reach the land of the Dutch, you must go that way, France will not be safe, nowhere will be safe for your kind now, travel well and prosper my friends" said Talan handing the reigns to William.

Miana came outside and tied the sacks to the horses saddles, she looked at William and smiled, the smile broke into Williams heart, her smile reminding him of a girl he once knew back in England, before he took his vows to God.

The small farm crept away into the distance as dust kicked up behind the Templar, speed was of the essence and haste was in their blood.

Months passed by and the weary travellers found themselves in the Germanic region, the town of Saarbruken stood beyond a dense forest "we must travel through the black forest and rest in the town" pointed out William gesturing toward the thicket of trees before them.

Geoffrey looked uneasy " can we not go around?" he asked "I fear there may be spirits in these woods" he was such a big man and Geoffrey was rarely afraid of anything but the forest was dark and so dense a man could throw an axe and never find where it landed.

William and Geoffrey tethered the horses to a nearby tree "we cannot take the horses further" said William "they won't make it they're exhausted". Cautiously the Templar's entered the trees, a giant oak loomed over them, it's branches reaching out to grasp unsuspecting travellers, the path was rugged and littered with fallen branches and tree trunks. Outlaws were rumoured to occupy this part of Germany and both Geoffrey and William kept one hand on the hilt of their sword.

Geoffrey stopped without warning, he held his hand up signalling for William to halt and listen, the wind sang ancient lullabies as it rustled through the leaves, there was no birdsong to accompany it however, this was what had caused Geoffrey to stop. "Do you hear that ?" he asked, William nodded "aye the birds do not sing, we have company" he remarked softly, as he began to unsheathe his weapon.

A group of men dressed in rags, wielding pitch forks and clubs ran out of the undergrowth and surrounded the Templar's. "What do you want! Do you not know we are knights of the Order?" demanded William angrily.

A small man stepped forward, his toothless grin making him look uglier than he actually was, long greying hair and a scruffy beard covered his features. "I thought it was obvious what we want" he laughed " and yes we know what you are and we know the king of France would pay a pretty penny for your heads" he continued.

He walked closer to the Templar's and was met by the cold steel of Williams blade "ah I see that we will not take you easily" said the small man taking a step back "perhaps we can save the blood and make a deal" he said rubbing his grubby chin in thought.

"We have no riches to give" said Geoffrey who had also unsheathed his sword, the small man smiled again "yes I realise that as knights Templar you have forsaken all worldly goods, however if you were to teach my men the art of the sword we shall give you safe passage through our forest" he said stepping to one side and motioning to his ragged companions, "we have no time to do this task" replied William "nor do I wish to give you the means to harm others" he continued stepping forward.

The small man shrugged his shoulders, "alas though my men do not know the art of the sword, they do know how to skewer a man with a fork or beat his brains out with a club". He nodded to a large set man who held a spiked club in his hand, the man leapt forward bringing the heavy looking weapon crashing down toward William.

Before the man's club could connect, William's sword found its place between his rib cage, the man fell to the ground with a noisy thump, the small man looked at William then at his fallen comrade "you just killed my brother" he snarled "get em boys leave none alive!" he shouted.

A battle ensued yet the bandits were no match for trained fighting men of the Order and soon all but the small man lay either dead or wounded on the forest floor.

William stuck his sword in the ground beside him and picked the small man up by the scruff of his neck.

"We do this for a living" he said removing the dagger from his belt and slitting the man's throat without a thought, he let his limp body drop to the floor and turned to Geoffrey "Search them for anything useful then we must go there may be more" Geoffrey didn't argue and rummaged through the bandit's pockets, finishing off any who were mortally wounded to save their suffering.

The forest seemed to go on forever as the two Templar's continued their journey to the coast and home to England's shore.

The Dutch were said to be more friendly toward the Templar, and the tiny fishing village of Maiden on the Netherlands coast was their destination before traversing across the treacherous North Sea. The village was at least another four weeks walk and they began to regret leaving the horses behind, their feet burning it was days before they rested again.

The castle of Bred-erode stood Three miles from the knights destination. The fortress held troops who were loyal to the King of France. Alverade Bred-erode resided inside the castle, the eldest of six brothers he had inherited the castle from his father after his death in 1285 AD. Alverade was a ruthless warrior and leader, his troops would follow any man whom paid the right price. Tonight though the castle rang with laughter and merriment as the occupants feasted.

A lone sentry stood guard upon the battlements, as he stood looking out over the land, he saw shadows moving slowly out of the trees. He didn't make a sound and acted as though he hadn't seen William and Geoffrey as they stepped cautiously through the dark marshes. The sentry walked slowly down the steps of the battlements and across the courtyard where a burly officer stood. "Sir there are men in the marshes should we send out a party to see what they are up to?" he asked, the officer put down the sharpening stone he had been using to re-edge his blade and called out an order. Within moments, a group of ten militia were stood to attention.

"There are men in the marsh, bring them back for questioning" barked the officer "and I want them alive", he added knowing his men to be as ruthless as the lord of the castle. Ten armed militia rode out of the castle gates and into the surrounding marsh, they were upon William and Geoffrey within minutes and despite their greatest efforts both men found themselves over powered by man and horse, tethered and gagged they were dragged into the castle courtyard.

"My name is Alverade Bred-erode and you are in my land now" said the lord of the manor as he stepped down the keep stairs and into the courtyard. "Tell me, is there any reason I should not kill you now, after all the King of France would pay a good price for you dead or alive" he sneered looking the Knights up and down He motioned to a soldier to remove their gags and stepped closer, William tried to stand up and was greeted by a soldiers boot "kneel in front of our Lord" he hissed.

Lord Alverade placed a hand on the soldiers arm " please there is no need to mistreat our guests" he smiled warmly and continued. "Besides I have a fate in store for these men which would be much more satisfactory".

Lord Alverade motioned to the officer to bring his sword, he took it and began to wave it around close to the Templar's faces, Geoffrey turned his head and looked at William "now?" he asked "NOW!" shouted William freeing his hands with a shard of glass from the ground.

Both men jumped up and grasped a sword each from an unsuspecting soldier Geoffrey lurched toward Lord Alverade who parried his blow with ease, spinning his blade around Geoffrey lunged again, this time his strike hit home slicing a thin line in Lord Alverade's cheek. Doing so made the Lord lose his temper, he thrust, parried and matched Geoffrey blow for blow, he ignored the line of blood dripping to the floor, and he brought his sword crashing down and into Geoffrey's shoulder blade.

Geoffrey let out a scream of pain and dropped his sword. William upon hearing his friends plight, ripped the guts from his opponent with a swift slash and ran to help, he was too late, Lord Alverade had slit Geoffrey throat and his body lay limp and lifeless in a pool of his own blood.

William stopped himself and listened to reason. On his own he couldn't take them all on, could he escape he wondered looking around at the large band of soldiers who were beginning to surround him, he spotted one of the horses a few feet away.

Somehow he found the strength to pick Geoffrey's body up and throw him over the horse before jumping on himself and heading for the open portcullis and the drawbridge, soldiers poured out of the castle behind him. As he raced through the marsh and on to the coast, but first he must lose his pursuers.

A group of trees lay ahead, the soldiers were close but he had gained a substantial lead. He headed for the copse of trees. The undergrowth was thick and William found it easy to hide himself and the horse within its confines, a safe haven until the soldiers pass by.

He waited for what seemed an eternity soothing the horse with his hand stroking her long mane so as to keep her from making a sound and giving his position away, the soldiers didn't come. "They must have lost our trail and headed another direction" whispered William to the horse, who whinnied softly and nodded her head as though agreeing. Cautiously William led the mare and Geoffrey corpse out of the woodland, he could smell the sea and taste salt on his lips. He was close and soon sand was beneath the horses hooves, this time it was wet sand.

The tide was on it's way out, "perfect timing" he thought."now all I need is a boat". As though by magic as he rounded a bend in the beach a small sail boat was moored, it's captain lay with his head on a small barrel his hat over his eyes, soft volcanic eruptions burst from his hairy nostrils. "Ahem!" coughed William.

The Captain didn't move. William stuck his boot out and pushed at the barrel watching it roll backwards and laughing as the Captain's head smashed against the sand awakening him instantly. "what the blazes, who are you, what do you want and why did you wake me up" demanded the stunned captain. "My name is William Lyvett, a knight of the Templar order, I seek passage for myself and the body of my friend to England, I must see he is buried in home soil".

The captain looked over at Geoffrey's lifeless body," aye I understand, my name is Captain Jules De'verne but you may call me Captain" he smiled a toothless grin. "Here use this to wrap your friend in" he said passing William a spare sail. "There isn't room for both of you aboard the ship" said the captain nodding toward the small boat. "We can fasten your friends corpse to the tow raft" he continued. Before long the small boat was crashing over the waves. The wind driving the sails, the boat drifted forward. A crudely made raft bobbed behind it tethered to the stern. Geoffrey was lashed tightly to it with rope, William watched the land disappear behind them as the sun began to sink, soon he would be home, soon he would be back in England.

2 TREASURES OF HOME.

September, 1308, the sun beat down as White cliffs came into view on the horizon. The open mouth of the river Humber awaited the small sail boat to drift along it's tidal flow. William and the Captain were both happy to see land before them. "We can't moor up at the main harbour Captain" said William adjusting his view. " I know not if the King of France has hands and eyes here yet". Several miles along the Humber the captain steered his vessel toward the shore.

"This will have to be the place I leave you Sir William, I wish you a safe journey my friend" he said as he helped William disembark and drag Geoffrey's body up the banking."Dear captain I owe you a great debt" said William shaking the captains hand " I bid you farewell".

William removed his tunic knowing that he must hide his identity if the rumours were true and stuffed it into a cloth bag. He lifted the dead weight of Geoffrey corpse over his shoulder and set off following the river West, his first destination was to be Fax-fleet where Geoffrey had been preceptor before he joined the crusades.

The village of Hessle was a picturesque location, perched on the shore of the Humber. Another days ride from Fax-fleet, this was as close as William could go tonight. The darkness encased him as he trudged along, his knees weakening beneath the weight of the body he carried. As he approached an elderly gentleman stepped out of one of the hovels holding a torch and shouted " you there, show yourself, who are you and what do you want? We are but simple farmers and have no wealth" he coughed violently clutching his chest as he did so.

William stepped into the light " My name is William, although Who I am is not important, I seek refuge for the night, I can not pay but I am willing to work for food and shelter" he offered as he lay Geoffrey's body on the muddy ground "what be that?" asked the old man gesturing toward the wrapped corpse. William sighed "that be a good friend whom I shall bury in Fax-fleet tomorrow day" he answered, the old man nodded in acknowledgement and beckoned for William to follow him inside.

The hovel was more of a roughly built mud and stone shack with a thatched roof, a fire pit in the centre "this is my daughter Jenny and my son David, my name is Anthony" said the old man pointing to a pretty dark haired girl in her mid twenties and a red haired boy who looked around Sixteen years of age.

William settled down for the night, safe in the knowledge he was back on English soil, the night passed by uneventfully and William was greeted the next morning by the smell of bacon cooking on the fire.

"Breakfast will be ready in a short while" said Jenny as she saw William rise " I hope you slept well Sir" she added dishing 4 slices onto a wooden plate and breaking a chunk of bread off. She passed the meal to him, smiled and said "enjoy" before skipping out of the door.

William ate the meal, savouring the salty flavour of the meat a flavour he hadn't tasted in such a long time. His plate finished he stood and went to the open door of the house, looking around he noticed Three more houses set to the east and between them a large garden area containing flowering vegetables.

"Ah good morning William I trust you slept well?" asked Anthony leaning on a stick by the garden fence. "Yes thank you my good man, and thank your daughter for the hearty breakfast, tis a long time since I ate so well", replied William stretching his arms.

"What chores do you wish me to do Anthony?" William asked walking out into the bright sunlight. Anthony stood and pondered the question. He then smiled "perhaps you could chop some firewood, the axe is by the barn" he replied gesturing to an even more run down building several hundred yards away, William nodded his acknowledgement and headed in the direction of the axe. Rested and feeling much more at ease from the nights sleep and the mornings meal.

William's strength had returned and it took only an hour to completely chop the large pile of logs into smaller pieces. He looked around to see if there were any more and satisfied the job was done returned to Anthony.

"Thank you for your hospitality" said William as he retrieved Geoffrey corpse. He glanced behind him as he left the Village behind.

It took William only a few more hours to reach the Village of Fax-fleet The stone hall of the Preceptory stood watch over the river bank. This however, was not his destination, but a small house on the outskirts. The door opened and a grey haired old women stepped to one side, beckoning for him to enter.

"It is a sad day when a parent outlives the son, it is a sad day when a comrade falls, but today we shall rejoice in the life of Sir Geoffrey Jolif, Templar, Lord of the realm, Son, we gather here to celebrate your life and know you shall find solitude in your death".

The Priest stepped back from the pyre "are you sure you would not prefer to have him buried on consecrated soil?" he asked the old woman. She shook her frail head.

"No despite Geoffrey's service to the church he was a believer in the old God's at heart and he would want it this way". She wiped a tear from her eye and turned to walk away as the flame was lit and William set alight to the funeral pyre. Thick black smoke bellowed up toward the heavens along with Geoffrey's soul.

"Sir William, if I may I would like a word" said the old woman as they returned to the small house. "You were the closest to a brother my son had, I am sure he would want you to have his horse" she smiled, William bowed his head and kissed the frail hand.

"Thank you Mrs Jolif I shall treat the horse with kindness and she shall serve me well for I have a mission to complete and must leave on the morrow". Mrs Jolif nodded her head as they entered the house. The evening was spent sat in quiet contemplation remembering a friend, a son, a life that had been hero, life taker, companion and confidant.

The morning was greeted with a gentle spray of rain which gave a shine to the world. William mounted the grey mare, whispering softly in her ear before digging his heels in and motioning the powerful beast North. He hadn't forgotten the letter nor the instructions given to him by the Grand Master. "Deliver this letter directly, it must reach Robert De Rygate before the end of the year" he had been told.

Robert De Rygate was the Preceptor at Copmanthorpe Preceptory. He was a tall man with long grey hair and beard adorning his head and face. He looked young for his Sixty Five years but his eyes told a different story. Robert was a trustworthy man and had been Preceptor at Copmanthorpe for many years. Respected throughout the county of Yorkshire he was also known as The Keeper of the Castle Mills at York.

Today Robert wasn't at home in Copmanthorpe, he had decided to go fishing and was sat by the river a mile north of the Preceptory when William arrived. A young boy of around Ten years old greeted him. " I am sorry but Sir Robert went fishing" he said as William began to dismount. "Where did he go fishing? I have an important delivery for him" said William mounting the horse again. The young boy scratched his head "ERM he said he was going to the river. I know his favourite spot I can show you" he said enthusiastically.

William lent down and offered his hand to the boy who grasped it tightly, with one swift pull the boy was seated behind William. "This way" said the boy pointing North.

"Come on you bugger, you won't escape me this time." SPLASH!! Robert fell face first into the fast flowing river, his stick rod floated past him. The large trout thrashing about, Robert picked himself up and raced after the stick. Catching up with it a few yards downstream, He pulled hard on the stick and was surprised to find the fish was still hooked.

Reeling the line towards himself he scooped the trout up into his arms, then waded back to shore. His clothes were dripping wet as he unhooked the fish and lay it on the bank.

Sitting down on the grass Robert gasped for air. It was then he heard the thunder of horse hooves and the shout of the young boy. " Sir Robert, Sir Robert we have an important delivery for you" he smiled waving his arm at the soaking man. William pulled the horse to a standstill and dismounted.

" I am Sir William Lyvett of Newlands, I bring you a message from the Grand Master, also I must speak with you about rumours I heard on my travels here". He reached into the bag and pulled out his Templar tunic, removing his dagger he slipped the blade between the lining slicing the lining open. An envelope dropped to Sir Robert's feet. Sir Robert picked it up.

"What is this?" he asked. William shrugged his shoulders, " I know not what the message contains" he said helping Sir Robert to his feet, the envelope gripped firmly in his hand. Sir Robert broke the wax seal and read the contents all the time muttering to himself "this can not be, the scoundrel" he turned to William with a grave look upon his weathered face.

"It seems the King of France has waged a war on our brotherhood, he accuses us of Witchcraft, Homosexuality, Heretics and worshippers of a false idol". He paused to gain his breath.

"He has sent word to our King via the pope, requesting all Templar be arrested". Robert sighed and passed the letter to William to read for himself. Shaking his head as he read the words.

William handed the note back to Robert and mounted his horse. "I shall request a meeting with King myself" he said pulling himself up into the worn leather saddle, Sir Robert shook his head. "No, no that task must lay with me, you ride to the other Preceptories and warn them of what we have learned" he said picking up the fish and his rod and heading back toward the Preceptory.

William made haste and visited each Preceptory in Yorkshire one by one relaying the message that the King of France was arresting their brethren and murdering them. It took him only a week to visit each village, eventually he found himself riding into his own village of Altofts and the nearby Newlands Preceptory of which he was the Preceptor.

He settled in at home and lay his boots beside the stone fireplace in the main hall, his feet ached almost as much as his heart. All the blood loss and for what? To be outlawed in every country? Was this really what he had fought for?

A few days later there was a knock at the Preceptory hall door and a young man entered, "Sir I bring you news from Sir Robert De Rygate" he handed a sealed scroll to William and left him to read.

'My dear William, I write to you with good news, our

King, Edward II has granted amnesty to the Templar in

Britain, he has no quarrel with us and has written to the

pope to tell him as such'.

William smiled, safe in the knowledge that he and his brotherhood were permitted to live as they did in their homes. For the first time in many a year William felt secure and began to let his guard down. He wandered around the local village as any free man would, although his sword always hung from his belt at the ready.

Four years of peace passed by in England for the Templar. Edward had defended their honour and written to the Pope in defence of the order, this was until he was advised that the property and lands of the order amounted to a vast amount of gold, jewels and Holy relics brought back from the Crusades.

The small Preceptory of Newlands stood over looking the River Calder South East of Wakefield.

None heard the rider approach. Only One saw the dust covering his tunic and the grave look upon his face as he delivered the news that the Templar were all to be arrested and tried.

"My good friend, I must advise you that resistance is futile, the King has made his wishes clear and those of us left are to be rounded up" said the dust covered knight. William held his head in his hands.

"Alas I thought my days of running and fighting were gone Stephen, how can Edward allow such a thing." Stephen De Radenache shook his head. " I know not why William, I do however have word that we must remove all holy relics from the Preceptories and hide them safe for the King will surely destroy them" replied Stephen pacing up and down the cold hallway.

"We shall gather those who remain and collect the treasures from each Preceptory" said Stephen.

Finally after a long silence between the two men William spoke. "We must take the treasures North and hide them, for if the king were to get his hands on the relics alone, who knows what power he would yield".

Stephen looked at William who nodded with approval. With that spoken, the two men departed. Taking with them all treasures from the Newlands Estate and travelling North then East before heading North once more.

It was late December when they finally reached the final Preceptory, the ground was hardened with frost and the trees were barren as were the fields. Little Ribston Preceptory was the furthest north.

The large cart drawn by three horses rumbled down the rough snow covered muck track. William and a band of six Templar escorted it into the village. They had been unchallenged in their quest and avoided capture by the Inquisition and the Kings soldiers by keeping to the offbeat tracks.

"This is the last of it" said a chubby balding knight as he threw a sack of gold coins onto the wagon. "So where will you be heading from here" he asked, knowing they would not tell. The question was more to pass the time than an enquiry.

"We shall take the treasure to a safe haven where the heavens meet the earth " replied William.

As night fell in around the Preceptory at Ribston the cart rumbled off into the darkness. Only two knights rode out with it, William and Robert.

They rode North East crossing the River Nidd at Ribston.

The wind howled through the trees lining the bank of the fast flowing water.

Knaresborough castle loomed on the hill in the distance, large wooden scaffold clung to the stonework. The King had ordered work to be done modifying the castle. The main Garrison had been re-stationed at Spofforth castle just South West of Ribston. Leaving a small garrison of soldiers to patrol the walls.

Hidden by a wall of trees along the river, the cart rumbled along undetected.

The Sun was at it's highest and it was quite warm now the wind had dropped. William heard a large grumbling sound. "I take it you are hungry brother Robert?" He chuckled as he saw the old man rubbing his groaning stomach. "yes William, perhaps we could stop for some lunch?" William nodded and seeing a small clearing ahead slowed the cart down to a standstill. "This will do just fine" smiled Robert clambering down and reaching into the back of the cart.

He removed a large sack containing bread and cheese and several bottles of mead.

Kingfishers dove for minnows, then perched on the outgrowing roots sticking out of the bank, brandishing their prey with pride.

As William and Robert tucked into their meal they watched the display of nature before them. Fish topped for flies and a feeling of peace washed over the men. The silence was broken by a loud scream nearby.

"Help! Leave me alone" shouted the victim as she was mauled to the ground by two burly looking soldiers.

William came running around the corner. A large chunk of bread still undergoing a good chewing in his mouth, he stopped sharply, cannoning into one of the men and sending him flying into the river.

Turning on his heels, William drew his sword and leapt toward the other soldier, the woman was backed against a large rock sobbing into her hands. "This is of no concern to you, move along now and I shall let you live" snarled the soldier drawing his sword. William let a sly grin creep onto his face. Closing his eyes he took a deep breath.

The soldier seeing William appear to be unguarded took this as an opportunity to lunge forward with his blade. Within a breaths moment William sidestepped and plunged his sword hilt deep into the soldiers chest. William let out a sigh and removed the weapon from the corpse wiping it on the tunic of his victim.

Placing the weapon in it's scabbard he stepped cautiously toward the woman. "Here let me help you" he said softly reaching out a hand to help her up. She took it gratefully. "Why were the soldiers chasing you?" he asked as they headed back to Robert and the cart.

" I stole some venison from the castle granary" she sniffed rubbing her nose on her sleeve. "Why did you steal the food? Does your lord not pay his subjects to work?" he asked passing her a small piece of cloth to wipe her eyes and nose with.

She nodded a thank you and replied. "I have not eaten for Three days, my father and brother were taken to the castle to work and did not return". She passed the cloth back to William who promptly refused and insisted she kept it.

"I went to the castle to find them but they weren't there, I saw the door to the granary and, well the rest you know" she continued. Robert stood to greet the newcomer. "What is your name child?" he asked seating her on a small rock and handing her a tankard of mead and a chunk of bread. The woman devoured the bread without a thought and washed it down with the sweet Ale.

"My name is Eleanor, I am the daughter of Edgar the stone mason of Scriven", she replied eventually. "I thank you for your kindness, and ask only for your names?" she added with a smile. "I am William Lyvett and this is my comrade Robert De Rygate". He omitted the part about them being Knights. Deciding that a small deceit was better than risking their mission. "I am grateful to you both for your help, I must find my father and brother though". She stood brushing the crumbs from her dress. "Perhaps we could accompany you" said Robert momentarily forgetting their mission.

William shot him a glance of disapproval and was relieved when Eleanor refused the offer. " Thank you but I am sure they will be safe" she smiled and left the two Templar by the river clearing. Neither saw glance inside the cart as she left. " It is time we moved onward William" said the old knight packing away the food remains.

Soon they were back on the track, the cart rumbling slowly beside them. The track hugged the contours of the river as it twisted and distorted through the valley. Hills on either side would make this a perfect place for an ambush.

William recognising the danger immediately placed his hand on the hilt of his sword. Large oaks replaced the smaller willows and soon a vast woodland bore home to the wanderers feet. The faint rumble of water rushing downstream could still be heard to their right and above this a sheer cliff acted as a wall. The scenery did not change for several miles until they eventually came back onto the river bank and a crossing North.

The water was shallow here and the cart had no problem navigating the small rocks and boulders laying beneath the surface. As they reached the far bank a shout alerted them.

"Halt I am to believe you have on your persons a vast amount of treasures, pray how did you come by such riches." The voice came from a well dressed gent mounted on a stunning chestnut mare.

"We are but poor monks delivering religious artefacts to the monastery at Leyburn" replied William, his head bowed. The horseman rubbed his bearded chin. "Hmm I see, may I have a look at these artefacts?" he asked dismounting and stepping toward the cart. William felt his hand drift toward his sword but stopped himself.

The man was alone it seemed, and relatively unarmed, save a small dagger in his belt. "Of course my lord" said Robert, reaching into the cart and retrieving a large piece of wood "this is a piece of the true cross of Jesus" he said making the sign of a cross on his chest and showing the man the plank. "and what of the gold I heard about?" he asked stepping even closer to the cart "nothing more than crucifix's and goblets for the monastery" replied Robert pulling the cloth over the cart and fastening the rope.

"You are aware that bandits operate in these woods." Said the man as he moved back to his horse. "I am certain we can handle any rabble" smiled William. "My name is John of Bardsey I am squire to Lord Gravestone of Knaresborough Castle" said the man stroking his mares mane. "I know the land between here and Allendale better than any hunter or trapper alive" he boasted. "Perhaps you could do with someone who knows the land in your party? I grow weary of squiring and wish to see adventure" he continued not waiting for the other men to speak he mounted his horse

" shall we go then?" he grinned. "You may escort us as far as Ripon then we part ways" said William climbing up onto the cart seat. He helped Robert up beside him and they followed John up the steep hill.

"So how did you know of our cargo?" asked William suspiciously, John smiled. "you helped my sister earlier today, Eleanor" he said. "She told me of the treasures you carry and asked me to guide you, I do so with honour and thanks" he bowed his head to William and Robert. Upon hearing this William relaxed a little and began to treat John with less distaste, even sharing a joke along the route, the three men laughed heartily as they travelled.

The journey North was uneventful and as they reached Ripon William whispered to Robert. "We are close to Penhill perhaps we should bed down there for the night." Robert nodded in agreement. "What about John, should we depart as agreed?" he asked glancing at the rider.

William thought hard and long before answering the question. "No I think he will be of use to us, we should ask him to escort us to Caithness the grand master said we would be safe there" His voice was firm as he spoke, yet it was comforting to Robert who knew the man by his side was of good judgement.

So it was agreed that the Squire would join them on their trip Northward. He just had to be told what their cargo really was, which could wait until they were comfortable at Penhill Preceptory.

"We are changing our plans slightly John" said William as they came out of the woodland and into wide open fields. "We shall bed down at the village of Penhill West of here, we ERM have a friend there who will give us food and shelter for the night, We insist that you join us before your journey home." John nodded his head. "Aye that would be a fair exchange for the horse as a pillow".

The shadow of Penhill Preceptory loomed into sight, no candles burned in the windows, the land around it was in darkness.

"Something is wrong" said William pulling the cart to a halt atop a hill overlooking the buildings. "Someone should be here", said Robert straining his eyes to see if he could spot any movement in the blackness.

"John may I borrow your horse to scout ahead?" asked William stepping down from the cart. "Of course" replied John dismounting and handing the reigns to him. "her name is Abnoba after the Celtic goddess of rivers and forests he added before William mounted the mare and headed toward the Preceptory.

The faint smell of smoke and charred meat filled his nostrils as he approached. This was a familiar aroma to a man of war. He dismounted Abnoba and tethered her to a nearby tree, slowly withdrawing his sword he stepped cautiously toward the doorway. He pushed the oak panels open revealing a sinister and stomach wrenching view. Six Templar's were crucified all along the walls large iron nails rammed through their hands and feet. Pools of blood stained the floor beneath them.

William sank to his knees placing his head upon the hilt of his sword he prayed for their souls before gently removing each from their humiliating death poses and laying them beside one another on the floor. He covered each face with a cloth then finding a torch he lit it and signalled his comrades.

"look a light" said John. "That's William" smiled Robert. "Come lets go to him."The cart rumbled down the hill and William came out to meet them holding three shovels.

"We have work to do before we settle" he said solemnly handing a shovel to each of them. Without asking why, both men followed him to the rear of the Preceptory and began to dig. "We need to dig six graves" William said as he finished his first hole it took the men several hours before they could bury the dead Templar's. As they eventually sat down around a small fire in the main hall none spoke of the horror that had befallen the Templar of Penhill.

Somewhat rested they awoke the next morning with a heavy weight on their hearts, "We must keep travelling North" said Robert as he pushed an apple down his throat more for substance than the taste. None felt like eating much this morning. William shook his head. "No we can not risk it now, the king has betrayed us. This is his doing." He said waving his hand around the up turned room. "For what reason would you say this?" asked John angrily.

John was an honest man and loyal to the crown. Anger boiled in his blood when he heard the words against his king. "Please settle yourself John" said William calmly placing his hand on John's arm. "You do not know of the kings plan for the Knights of the Temple."

He lowered his head and breathed in deeply hoping that he would not have to kill John as he had become to like the young man. "What plan? What is he talking about?" asked John looking toward Robert who shot a glance at his comrade. William nodded his head "it is all good tell him" he sighed. "The king has declared all Templar's outlaws for crimes they did not commit on the say of the king of France, the Templar's are being hunted and murdered across the known world".

Robert took a drink and wiped his bearded chin "this my brother John is why myself and William are taking the Preceptory treasures away to be hidden." John sat and contemplated the information he had just been told. Could this be true? Would the King really betray the Templar this way? Who else would murder monks?

These and other thoughts swam around John's head until he finally stood and spoke. "Your honour speaks for itself in the deed you did for my Sister." He began looking directly at William.

"For this I am at your service until the debt is repaid." He bowed his head and offered his blade to William. "Thank you John, I understand that you are loyal to the King and I respect that loyalty in a man." William replied as he helped John up from his knees. "The fact that we are Templar Knights should not come between us!" he continued turning to begin packing food for the journey ahead. "We should take what we can carry the journey ahead is a long one." said Robert handing a discarded sword to John.

The sun was high in the sky this day. A small cart carrying two Templar knights and a kings ransom of treasures trundled along the rough track way. Ahead a lone rider led them across the precarious moorland. "We must avoid Ripon" said John pointing to the North. "our best route would be East and across the River Ure then head North from there" he added as he spurred his horse toward the East.

Borough-bridge lay in the distance, the closest crossing of the River Ure, from there it would only take a few days heading North to reach Northumberland, then on to the border. The small village was busy this day, a market was taking place in the Village Hall. It would be simple to slip through the bustle with the cart and they were not challenged until they reached the bridge across the river.

"Stop there" ordered the sergeant beckoning for the cart to halt. William and Robert glanced at one another and readied themselves for the attack. The burly sergeant stepped forward "what's in the cart?" He asked going to the rear of the vehicle. He lifted the cloth and then withdrew his sword. "In the name of the King I order you to step down from the cart" he shouted. Two more guards stepped toward the cart.

William and Robert obeyed not wanting to cause a scene in the busy village. "Now where did you get these items?" asked the sergeant rummaging through the artefacts and chests of coins. The knights did not answer. John dismounted his horse "These men are with me Sergeant!" He said stepping boldly toward the soldier. "And who the ell are you?" the Sergeant asked replacing a large crucifix back onto the cart.

"I, Sir am Squire to Lord Gravestone of Knaresborough." He handed a sealed scroll to the Sergeant who glanced at it then handed it back apologetically. "I am sorry sir please continue." he gestured toward the bridge.

It was another Four miles to the next crossing at Asenby over the River Swale then another Eleven to Northallerton. The going was rough along the dirt tracks as the rain began to fall soaking the companions to the skin. Darkness began to settle in as they reached the gates to the town.

John once more used his seal of Knaresborough to gain access to the town and a warm bed for him and his companions for the night. " I shall sleep with the cart!" said William laying himself beneath a blanket on the straw in the stables. "All well and good for you my friend, I however am looking forward to a mug of ale and a warm soft bed." smiled Robert leaving with John.

Somewhere in the distance a cockerel let out it's morning call. The sound echoing throughout the market town as stall holders busied themselves setting up shop. William awoke to his friend Robert shaking him. "William! William! Wake up it is time we left, before any of the kings soldiers grow suspicious of us". William stood and yawned loudly. "Yes my friend I shall ready the horses and the cart." he replied stretching his arms out front.

John had already taken the liberty of saddling his own horse and was waiting outside the stable as the cart was pulled through the open door and into the busy street. They made their way through the narrow streets, carefully avoiding the castle a hooded figure stepped out in front of the cart.

The horse stumbled backwards in fright and it took all William's strength to hold the beast. "Whoa there!" he called out leaning over to pat the horses mane. "My apologies good sirs" said the hooded man lowering his gaze to the floor.

As he did so his long cowl shifted to one side. There, hung on his belt, was a sword. A sword that William recognised instantly embellished with a cross upon the hilt. A sword of the Knights Templar.

"You there" called William as the man began to walk away. "Please come let us talk, I feel we may have business to discuss." continued William stepping down from the cart. The hooded man lifted his head. His bearded face weathered and worn.

Beneath the man's kind brown eyes William knew this was a member of his brotherhood. "Pray, what would a merchant have to discuss with an old drunk like me?" asked the hooded man. William took the man by the arm and led him between two buildings. "I saw your blade!" he said looking straight into the man's eyes. "We are the same!" he continued showing the hilt of his sword to the man. "my name is William Lyvett of Newlands." He held out his hand and the man shook it gently.

"I am Jauferre De St Clair brother in law to the grand master" replied the man. "Come, we are not safe here. Although the kings army is in Scotland, he has spies all around. "He led William back out of the alleyway and beckoned for him and his companions to follow.

"Oi where are you going" shouted a guard as they reached the North gate. "oh sir I thought it best I should leave town I drank too much at the Inn and fear I may be a little drunk." Jauferre fell into the guard the stench of stale ale drifted up his nose and he pushed Jauferre to the floor. "Go on get out of here!" he said planting his boot firmly against Jauferre rear.

"Thank you! Thank you kindly sir." said Jauferre bowing his head and heading out the gate. William and his friends carried on through the gate as Jauferre put on his pantomime. moments later he ran up and joined William and Robert on the cart. " We will be safe in the woodland at Upper Bonville." he said pointing toward a large expanse of woodland ahead of them.

Large green oaks towered above them as they rode into the woods. "Are you sure we will be safe in here? What about bandits?" asked Robert nervously. "Bandits stay clear of this area for fear of ghosts." laughed Jauferre. "Ghosts?" asked John nervously as he rode beside them. "Aye lad the spirits protect us through this land." "Just ahead here!" continued Jauferre pointing to a clearing.

As they approached there was a shout " who goes there" came the voice. "It is I Jauferre I bring some friends." Jauferre clambered down from the cart and greeted the newcomer. "my friends let me introduce you to my brothers in arms." He gestured around the clearing at a group of three heavily armed knights. The tunic of the Templar still worn proudly.

A hog roasted on the open fire and ale was passed around as the small group of Knights feasted through the night. William recalled the story of how he, Robert and John had ended up where they were as their companions sat and listened intently.

"And so we must protect these treasures with our lives and deliver them to a safe haven in the North" he finished. Each man looked toward his brother and nodded. Jauferre stood with sword in hand. "As Brothers of the Temple we shall stand by your side and deliver these holy relics to a safe place. we must travel to Caithness where my castle will be the final resting place of the artefacts" he finished.

He raised his mug and downed the ale in one sweep. "Thank you my friends" began William. "It will be a long journey and we must avoid the English armies". A small stocky man spoke up. "I hear that Robert the Bruce is sacking the English in the North." He rubbed his stubbly chin. "Perhaps he shall keep them busy enough not to notice a few old Knights slip by eh."

There was a cheer of "AYE" and the clinking of mugs. "Tonight we feast and tomorrow we ride" shouted Jauferre. There was much merriment in the camp as the stars danced in the velvet darkness watching over the Knights as they feasted.

The seasons began to change. Winter would soon settle it's bitter chill across the land. As the Knights rode North they reached a small cave carved into the cliff side at Doddington. "We shall rest here for the winter months" said William leading the cart and horses into the deep cavern.

"What about food and water?" asked John knowing that their provisions would last only a few more days. "We can hunt in the forest and perhaps barter for other goods we may need to keep us going at nearby villages" said Robert dragging a small dead tree toward the centre of the cave.

"That my friend is a good idea" smiled William patting the old man on the shoulder. " Come John we need wood for bows and iron for arrows" said Jauferre grabbing the squires arm and leading him out into the cold wind.

 The small stocky man whom had spoken of the Bruce was a skilled blacksmith by trade and knew how to make any weapon in the known world. David Beaumont was his name he had travelled from Southern France to escape the Inquisition along with his younger brother Stefan and of course their friend Jauferre De St Clair.

They were among One Thousand Knights who had escaped from France. They had set sail along with an armada of ships carrying the Knights and all their treasure. A fierce storm separated their ship from the fleet. They ran aground and the three were the only survivors.

No one knew what had happened to the rest of the fleet but the plan was to head North to Scotland and meet at St Clair castle in Caithness. This would have to wait, as travelling through the mountainous region was even more treacherous than normal. Bandits operated in the lawless region not to mention the weather which froze the ground beneath their feet and covered the land in a thick blanket of snow.

3 THE BRUCE

The Templar's days were spent hunting for Deer, Rabbit, Pheasant and grouse. They would then take it in turns to visit one of the local villages and trade the meat and skins for grain and mead. This went on for several months, the winter was unusually harsh and showed no sign of spring. "We must make haste North" chimed up Jauferre one day. The statement came out of nowhere. "We can not risk it in this weather!" said Robert knowing he was too frail to battle the elements.

"I heard talk in Kimmerston that the Bruce is heading to Bannockburn to meet the English army" said William changing the subject. His companions looked at him. "And what has that to do with us?" asked Stefan who was usually the quiet one of the group. "Not a thing" said William gulping down his drink"

"However" continued William. "The English will be busy with the Bruce which will give us the perfect opportunity to slip by unnoticed." He smiled and sat by the open cave doorway staring out into the blank canvas of white. Months had turned into endless repetitive days until finally the snow began to melt. Snowdrops appeared in small groups around the woodland, it was time to leave their safe haven.

The hills of Northumberland were an unforgiving barren wasteland.

Since the Romans left, Hadrian's wall lay in ruins. A lifeless scar on the landscape. It's forts now taken over by sheep and Bandits alike.

Wolves prowled in the shadows. Following the group as they could smell food. John was the first to catch a glimpse of the small pack of greys about a hundred yards behind them. He rode quickly to the front of the cart to warn William.

Before he reached the cart there was a cry behind him. David's horse was brought down by the pack. Stefan seeing his brother in trouble doubled back. Sword in hand he struck sending the larger of the wolves spinning on it's heels, he rode around the pack then back toward his brother who was fighting off two of the animals. Reaching down he grasped David's arm and swung him up behind him leaving the stray wolves to rip David's dead horse to pieces. The horse was a good distraction and soon the group found themselves approaching an old Roman fort.

Housteads Fort was all but in ruin. A few of the buildings had new thatch on them and smoke bellowed through the roof. Somebody was home. The question was, bandits? Or farmers? The answer soon became clear as they entered the gateway.

Sheep and cattle were penned in close to the houses. A young man in his Twenties stepped out of the largest building. "What do you want?, who are you?" he demanded removing a rusty sword from its sheath. He took a step toward the knights.

"We are but humble monks seeking shelter for the night" said William halting the cart beside the man. "Monks eh? Those two look like Templar to me I know that symbol on their tunics" replied the young man. David and Stefan looked nervously at William who shook his head not wanting to fight this simple farmer.

He smiled. "yes my friend you are correct they are Templar's and they are escorting precious artefacts, religious artefacts of great importance." He stepped down from the cart and pushed the young man's sword to one side.

"Then I suppose you may bed down in the barn for the night" replied the young man knowing he couldn't best the Knights in a fight. "But you be gone by the morning" he continued spitting onto the ground and chewing on a piece of straw. "I want no quarrel with the King" he said turning and heading back into the house.

The straw was soft and made a good bed for the Knights and their horses. The walls of the stable kept out the bitter wind which blew across the hills, battering the age old stone of the wall.

It had been Seven years since the King of France had declared the Templar heretics. Five years since the pope disbanded the order. It had taken a long time to travel the distance they had and the cart and roads seemed to be the only home they knew. Now they saw freedom beckoning to them as the snow topped mountains of the Scottish Lowlands came into sight.

Edinburgh was only Sixty Five miles away. There they would cross the Firth of Forth. It took almost a week to navigate the hills choosing to stay away from the main roads and tracks. Their only enemies here were the wolves and Bandits who operated in the area or were returning from raiding the English villages on the border. The city of Edinburgh was a maze of high built compact homes.

The streets gave the stench of urine and excrement thrown from windows high above them. The Four Knights and John headed toward the castle in the hope they would find solace there. Before they reached the base of the castle they were stopped by an elderly man. "Please stop, do not go to the castle" he said nervously.

"The English hold the castle" he continued. "Come I shall lead you to a safe place." William stopped the man in his tracks. "Wait, who are you and why should we trust you?" he asked. The old man smiled "you are knights of the temple order, are you not?" he asked pointing to David and Stefan's tunics.

"Those are dangerous garments to wear around here" he added. "If you wish to be safe you will trust me, come". He beckoned for them to follow him and began to walk ahead. William thought about their situation. The English held the castle and the old man was right the tunics of his fellow Templar would attract attention. He motioned for the horses to move and they followed the old man through the streets and away from the City.

Arthur's seat, as the hill was called, an extinct volcano on the outskirts of the City. As they reached the summit they were greeted by the sight of a large body of men. Two of them stepped forward Claymores in hand. "Who are these men?" asked one of them in a broad accent. "Ti okay Jack these are Templar knights as much enemies of the King as we are" replied the old man.

"Templar's ya say?" said Jack running his grubby hands through his thick matted red hair. "ya come to join the brawl?" he asked nudging John with his elbow as he walked around the men and the cart. "We were going to seek shelter at the castle" replied William. "Well to do that ye going to have to help us" said the old man.

"My name is Thomas Randolph the Earl of Moray" he said holding his hand out for William to shake. "And tonight we lay siege to the castle and take it back fer Scotland and the Bruce" he continued. "will ye give your sword to the cause?" he asked.

William looked around at his companions. "myself and my friends would be glad to offer our services, however Robert and John must stay out of harms way" he said gesturing to his friend and the Squire. "That is good" said Thomas. "Come I shall share our plan with you and your colleagues" he said leading William, David and Stefan into a large tent.

As night fell Twenty Seven Scots and Three Templar Knights followed a man by the name of William Frances toward the castle walls.

William Frances was a member of the Castle garrison who held no love for the King of England. He led them along a narrow path to a section of the wall which could be scaled with ease. Ropes were thrown and the Thirty men clambered up the stonework and over the battlements.

It didn't take long to overpower the few soldiers garrisoned inside and Edinburgh fell to the Scots once more. A beacon was lit and the rest of Thomas's men accompanied by Robert and John leading the cart and horses entered the castle gates. A warm bed and hearty meal awaited them all that night and with full stomachs they slept peacefully in the barracks.

There was a shout in the early hours "come quick I have found prisoners" shouted a scruffy looking young man. William and Thomas jumped up swords in hand and followed the man down into the dungeons. In the dimly lit cavern below the castle Forty men were chained to the walls. Their tunics unmistakable.

These were more brothers of the Order. William and Thomas hasted no time in unshackling the men and helping them to the courtyard and fresh air above. "Thank you, I am Henry Douglas, these are my men." William shook Henry's hand. " I am William Lyvett preceptor of Newlands" he replied. "And this is Thomas Earl of Moray" he said pointing to his companion. "We took the castle this eve" said Thomas helping another knight out of the dungeon.

The morning mist hung low around the castle. Cowering over the town with it's damp claws. Forty Four Templar's rode out of the castle that day. Led by William and Robert on the cart and the Squire John by their side.

The small army headed toward the estuary of the Firth of Forth there they would take the ferry across to Kirkaldy. The harbour was quiet as they arrived, the large ferry barge stood silent moored up to the bank.

"Hello" shouted William. "Ferry Master we wish to cross" he continued as a dark figure emerged from within a small hovel. "Alright, Alright, I'm coming" he said. "It will cost for so many men and horses" he said rubbing his chin and eyeing up the small army of Knights with Red crosses on their tunics.

William reached into the cart and pulled out a handful of silver coins. He poured them into the Ferry Masters hand. "Will this cover it?" he asked.

The Ferry Master smiled and beckoned for the men and horses to board the Ferry. There was a cold breeze on the river as they slowly drifted across. It took almost Thirty minutes for the old Ferry Master to pull the barge and it's load to the far bank and he was relieved when they finally reached their destination. "Good day to you sir" said Robert to the Ferry Master as they trundled off the barge and on to dry land. Followed closely by the army of Templar knights.

The small bay of Dalgety was spotted with small houses belonging to the local fishermen. In the distance the ruins of Incolm Abbey loomed on the island amidst the low fog over the Forth. A dark reminder of what the English King was capable of inflicting. As the group rode Northwards they came across a large expanse of water. Loch Leven had stood as an ancient pool of crystal clear water for centuries.

Now perched on an island several hundred metres away from the bank, a large tower house stood. Surrounded by thick stone walls, it was an almost impenetrable Fortress. A small jetty jutted out from the solace of the stone. Seeing the small army of knights gathered on the shore one of the castle guards called for his master.

"Sire come quick I think the English may be attacking again" he shouted down the corridor. A man with white hair and a long white beard appeared on the battlements. "It may look that way, but why do they not attempt to cross?" he asked watching the knights intently.

William glanced around and spotted a small boat tethered to the banking. "I shall speak to the lord of this manor, alone" he said untying the line and settling down with oars in hand.

"Be wary William, we know not if this is English ruled or Scot" said Robert placing his hand on Williams shoulder. The old Knight had become quite fond of William and the feeling was mutual. "Do not worry yourself my friend" smiled William digging the oars into the deep water he rowed toward the wooden jetty.

"Who are you and what do you want?" shouted the Lord of the manor perched on his battlements. Militia stood either side of him, pikes in hand. "Are you English or Scots?" replied William. "And what does that matter?" said the Lord beginning to grow impatient. "It matters a great deal for the reason we are here" said William mounting the Jetty and tying the boat beside another.

"I am Sir John Comyn Lord of this manor and I am Scottish through and through" shouted the Lord proudly.

"Then we are allies, I am William Lyvett Knight of the Temple of Solomon and those are my brothers in arms on yonder bank" he replied. The gate opened and Sir John stepped out to greet William.

"I heard that your order had been disbanded" he said shaking William's hand. "Aye you speak the truth sir, we are the last of our brotherhood and we seek food and shelter" he replied following the Lord up the staircase and into the main hall.

"I shall send boats for your friends" said Sir John beckoning to a pretty young girl in rags. She smiled and bowed her head before running off to inform the sergeant at arms to send for Williams comrades.

Before long all were enjoying a lavish feast. As they drank and ate, the door to the main hall flew open. A young messenger entered the hall. Breathless, he dropped to his knees, a scroll held in his hand. Two large men helped the young lad up and he handed the scroll to Sir John.

"It appears the Bruce is ordering all troops to Stirling he aims to meet the English for one final battle" said Sir John reading the scroll aloud. "Ready the men for tomorrow we march to Stirling" he ordered. His men finished their drinks and settled down for the night. "So my friend will you join us?" Sir John turned toward

William awaiting an answer. William thought for a moment, he knew they had to get the artefacts to safety yet in his heart he ached for revenge. The cruel murder of his brothers could not go unpunished. In the eyes of God he was the hand of justice.

He turned to face Sir John, "Aye Sir John we will join you, but first I must ask a favour." He felt uncomfortable bringing another outsider in on the secret of what they were guarding. Feeling that he had no other choice, he told Sir John of the treasures. "And so you see we must hide these artefacts in a safe haven" he finished. Sir John thought for a moment then replied. "Have your men take the treasure down into my dungeon, you shall leave your own personal guards to protect it until your return." he smiled and picked up his beaker finishing the contents.

William stood and walked to Robert and the Squire John. "My friends, tomorrow, myself and the other Templar's will be joining the Scots to battle the English at Stirling." Robert smiled it had been a long time since his sword had tasted blood.

"I need you and John to stay here with the treasure until I return" continued William laying his hand on his friends shoulders. "But we can fight" said John, angry that William wished to leave him behind. "yes I know you can fight my friend, however I need good honest men to guard the treasure." John understood and he and

Robert resigned to being guardians of the artefacts along with Stefan, David and Jauferre.

It took a days hard march to reach Stirling Bridge. As they marched into the town they were greeted by bands of Highlanders wavering their claymores and pikes in the air when they saw the Templar crosses. "We cannae lose now we have Templar's on our side" said one young warrior to his friend as the knights rode past.

Stirling castle stood proudly upon its high cliff. A major seat for Scotland, it was currently occupied by the English who were awaiting Edward's reinforcements.

As William and Sir John rode up to the siege camp below the castle they were followed closely by the Thirty Five Templar knights and One Hundred of Sir Johns men. A short dark haired, yet well dressed man with closely cropped beard stepped out of a lavish tapestried tent.

"Ah Sir John I am glad you joined us, and I see you have brought more than we bargained for" said the man eyeing William up and down. William now wore his tunic and stood proudly baring the symbol of the Templar Knights. "Yes Sire this is William Lyvett of the Knights Templar, And this is our King Robert the Bruce" continued Sir John introducing the two men.

William lowered to one knee and bowed his head against his sword hilt. "We are at your service your majesty" he said lowering his eyes from The Bruce's gaze.

"Please stand on this day we are brothers in arms and as such we are equals on the battlefield" said Robert flicking his hand upwards motioning for William to stand. William sheathed his sword.

"Come, follow me and we shall discuss the mornings campaign" said Robert leading them inside the tent. The other Knights busied themselves tending the horses and sharpening their steel blades. William stood by the war table with Robert the Bruce and several other Knights.

"How many men do the English have?" he asked. Robert called to a young lad. He spoke to him too quietly for William to hear and watched him run off toward the hillside. "We shall find out" smiled Robert as they waited the return of the spotter. Within the hour the Spotter returned to the camp. "Sire they have a vast army of around Eighteen Thousand, at least Five Hundred of these are Knights" he said gasping for air.

"Thank you James you are dismissed" he said tossing a silver coin to the boy. "We are no match with our Seven Thousand" said a burly gent stepping out of the darkness. "We are out numbered and out matched, we must ask for terms" he said banging his fist down on the table.

Robert's face changed from complacent to anger. "We shall do no such thing" he shouted returning the fist banging. "you of all people Moray should want the freedom of our country" snarled Robert gripping the man by his shirt. He threw the man to the ground and turned back to the map on the table. "There is an old Roman road which crosses the Bannockburn, this is where Edward's reinforcements will cross" said Robert,

He pointed to an expanse of woodland. "We will position troops in the trees along this road" he continued with a smile. "The English will not be able to fight in such close conditions" William nodded in agreement. "How wide is the road at the crossing?" he asked. "Around Forty Yards " said one of the other knights stood around the war table.

"This is my brother Edward" said Robert motioning toward the speaker. "Edward has been laying siege to Stirling for a year now" he said disappointedly. "The English have agreed to surrender if their King does not send reinforcements" continued Edward much to the distaste of his brother.

"We can not let the English get near to the castle" replied Robert, his voice now calm. "No it would be wiser to take them by surprise as they traverse the woodland road" he said. "For now though we must rest" he added holding his hand forward to show his comrades the way out. One by one they left The Bruce alone with his thoughts.

Fifteen hundred heavily armoured Knights on horseback rode toward the Bannockburn crossing. With the road being so narrow King Edward's army was stretched thin and snaked it's way along the track only Ten men breadth. As the Knights reached the tree line they were accosted by a wall of spears.

Robert's men had being trained with discipline and although they were seasoned warriors with claymore and axe, their main weapon of expertise was the spear. As affective against horse as it was against man, King Edward's knights soon found themselves bested by the Schiltrum.

The Bruce was ahead of his army organising the troops. One of King Edward's lone knights spotted The Bruce to one side and thought this was to be his moment of Glory. Sir Henry De Bowen charged. His horse galloped toward Robert The Bruce.

It would be his undoing. As he reached the Bruce, Robert arose out of his saddle and swung his small battle axe with such force that it crushed Sir Henry's skull. His limp, lifeless body fell from his horse and Robert wiped the blood splatters from his face.

Before long the Schiltrun's of men wielding spears were chasing the remainder of King Edward's Knights

South.

Now it was William and his comrades turn. They sped their horses into action following the English knights closely. Before the English cavalry reached the church they were stopped by another wall of spears. Soon all the English knights had fallen or retreated.

Night fell around the Scots camp. The English cavalry had retreated to the nearby marshes. The rest of their army stranded at the far side of the Bannock Burn. The decision to split their forces had proven drastic for the English and victorious for the Scots. That night a deserter arrived in the camp and relayed the news that the English were separated.

Robert was to take advantage of this news and leaving William and the cavalry in the woodland he marched his army forward. Stopping only to lead his men in prayer. Robert's Schiltrun's began to advance toward the English cavalry.

The knights in the camp could not believe their eyes, infantry men marching on cavalry? Surely this could not be? Seeing the advancing infantry the English Knights sped their horses toward them and up the hillside. Unwillingly sandwiching themselves between a dense woodland and a river.

Ahead of them the walls of spears. In such a compact area the Knights found their horses useless. They were forced back onto the marshlands. As the cavalry retreated, arrows rained down on The Bruce's infantry.

All along William waited hidden in the dense forest. Once the first barrage of arrows had loosed William gave a battle cry. He and Five Hundred mounted Knights charged at the Archers, scattering them like grain. The Scots had the advantage now.

As they marched forth with spears in hand, William and his Knights rode up behind the wall of men. A wall which now stretched the width of the battlefield.

The English found themselves with their backs to the Bannockburn. A few brave Knights charged forward into the Scottish ranks only to be cut down and trampled upon. What was left of King Edwards' army was forced into the river or lay dead beneath the Scottish feet. Of Those who made it into the river few made it out alive as they were cut down by Robert's men.

The English Infantry did not learn of the slaughter until an hour later. The battle was over and their comrades lay dead in the heather.

With tails between their legs King Edward and the remainder of his army turned and headed South for the English border. The battle was over as was the war, Scotland was now a free country. With the battle of Bannock Burn over William looked around to find Sir John.

4 THE SOLACE OF THE HIGHLANDS

"Thank You William, you fought well" said Robert shaking the Templar's hand. "you and your brotherhood shall always be welcome in Scotland" he continued. "now please Kneel" he said removing his sword.

"I appoint thee Knight protector of Scotland, arise Sir William Lyvett" said Robert placing the blade on each of William's shoulders. William stood up and thanked the king. "I must bid you farewell" he said nodding to Robert. The road back to Leven Castle was solitude compared to the blare of battle.

Inside Leven castle William was reunited with Robert and Squire John. "My friends it is good to see you" he said sitting by the fire with them and sharing a bottle of mead. "So what was it like?" asked squire John. "It was like all other battles, blood and more blood" sighed William not wanting to discuss the death of men.

Jauferre entered the hall from the chilly night wind. "Brr tis a cold one tonight" he said warming himself by the flames. "Thank you" he said as he took the mead offered to him, he gulped the sweet ale down and handed it on.

"So, when do we expect to head North?" he asked. William was beginning to find the question annoying. "We need to rest" he said taking another drink "yes, yes of course I was just curious as to when I would be home with my family" smiled Jauferre seating himself beside Squire John.

"You have a family?" enquired William knowing his order were forbidden to take part in carnal activity choosing a life of celibacy instead. "Yes, my brother he can not look after himself and I have been away for too long" said Jauferre.

"My sister was once married to the Grand master before he took his vows" he said staring into the fire. "Now she looks after Harold, he is my twin brother yet has the mind of a small child" he sighed. "It is now my turn to look after him so Alice may have her own life once more" he finished his story and looked around awaiting a reaction. There was none, there was nothing anyone could say but hold admiration for the Warrior who was to become a nurse maid.

William handed him the mead. "Here you need to drink more" he laughed. Jauferre laughed along with him and took another gulp of the liquid. "So William would you care to tell us your story?" asked Jauferre scraping something unpleasant off his boot and into the fire pit. The substance hissed and bubbled before dissolving. William shook his head. "Alas there is not much to tell" he said staring at the bubbling sap. "I am certain you were not always a Templar" said Squire John joining in the conversation.

"No I was once a land owner, I held lands at Altofts as far West as Walton and North of Wakefield." He spoke softly. "I was once married but that was before...." He broke off choking on the words "before she was killed" he added downing the rest of the mead. The other men in the room all stayed silent, except Robert who spoke before thinking. "Who killed her?" he asked.

John and Jauferre shot him an uneasy glance and he shrugged his shoulders as if to say "you were all thinking it, I just said it". William saw the glances and spoke up. "It is okay, it was a long long time ago. I had just turned Twenty and inherited my fathers lands." he reached by his seat and retrieved another bottle of mead. He poured some into a beaker and passed the rest around.

Shadows danced on the walls, marionettes in the flames cast them. William began to tell his tale of love and death. "Her name was Sarah she had the most beautiful blue eyes, like Sapphires." his mind began to drift to memories of the day they wed.

"We were young and in love. We were married in the spring and all seemed well with the world." The beaker of mead trembled in his hands as he spoke. "Then they came, one day while I was out hunting, Three men." "They took my wife, her dignity, her life." He felt a tear drift down his cheek and wiped it away quickly.

"I am sorry my friend" said Jauferre placing his hand on Williams arm. "we have all suffered and lost, some heavier than others" he said topping up William's drink. "So my friends that leaves just you young Squire and Robert" continued Jauferre looking at John and the old man. Robert shook his head "oh my story would take all week to recite" he said making the men laugh.

"No, I think we should hear the young Squires story" he said nudging John. "Well there isn't much to tell, my father is a stone mason. I did not want to follow his work and so became a Squire at Knaresborough castle." he shrugged his shoulders.

"Other than that no women, no brothers or sisters who need help" he shot a glance at Jauferre and William hoping he had not spoken out of term. Neither man seemed to have noticed. The night drew in around the band of Knights. Soon they were all asleep and in the morning they would ride for St Clair Castle and solitude from the screams of battle and death.

The sky was a deep blue and cloudless. A rare day in the Highlands of Scotland. No wind blew, yet it was still chilly compared to the deserts that William remembered clearly in his nightmares. Soft heather, like sponge beneath the horses hooves, made the travel slow.

None of the Knights seemed to mind as they marvelled at the beauty of the mountains. John rode up to the cart and pointed toward a group of trees. "Over there, I see deer" he smiled. "is anyone hungry?" he asked. Robert who always thought of his stomach first and foremost replied. "Aye food would be good right now, come William we have covered a fair distance this morning let us break for food." he held his hand up to halt the procession behind them.

The knights tethered their horses to nearby pine trees and several of them, with John, set off to capture their prey.

The men stalked the magnificent beasts through the woodland before choosing their spot down wind so as not to alert the deer with their stench. "You take the shot" said a large heavy set knight handing his long bow to John.

John drew back the string. The arrow wobbled slightly until he breathed in. Slowly he breathed out and let loose the arrow. Straight and true it found it's target between the Deer's front legs. Piercing its heart and killing the magnificent beast instantly.

A small fire burned back at the make shift camp and soon the aroma of roasting venison filled the occupants noses. Their stomachs rumbled at the aroma. The meat was tender and juicy and soon they were all tucking into a hearty meal. "so how far is St Clair Castle?" asked John chewing on a chunk of meat.

Jauferre spat a charred piece out of his mouth before replying. "It is around half a days ride to St Johnston and from there another one hundred and Fifty miles to Caithness." "So another four or five days ride" said John helping himself to another piece of meat.

The defences of the town of St Johnston stood in ruin. Ordered destroyed by the Bruce, many years before. This was to stop the English taking the town once more. The few people left living there were busying themselves with day to day chores. The fresh smell of bread came from a local bakery as did the unmistakeable aroma of hops from a brewery.

"We should bed down here for the night" said Jauferre leading his men to the stables, then on to the local tavern.

The dimly lit inn held the stench of stale beer and smoked fish. Even William felt at ease knowing the treasure was being closely guarded by four of his brethren. He settled in for the evening enjoying the mead and music.

Rain began to fall, as it often did in these parts. The large drops crashing into the roof of the inn like stones being thrown from a mountain crag. William awoke sharply at the noise.

He saw the daylight outside and raised himself from the comfort of the cot. His head began to pound like a funeral drum. "Too much mead my friend?" smiled Robert sat by the window. "Aye I fear I may be getting too old for such merriment" remarked William as he dressed himself.

The streets were awash with mud as they arrived outside the stables. The Four Knights who had stood watch that evening yawned and mounted their steeds. They were used to going without sleep and endured the tiredness venturing onwards.

The wet weather didn't seem to show any signs of letting up as the band of Knights followed the path along the River Tay. Another days ride and they found themselves by Loch Ericht and time to make camp again.

A small group of the knights split off to go fishing and as they sat by the side of the loch with sticks in hand they talked, no one at the camp could hear what was said but words of treachery were rife.

After a meal of Salmon caught in the Loch, and bread bought from the bakery in St Johnston, the Knights bedded down for the evening. Robert had insisted on being guard that night along with Three Knights he did not know well. Darkness enfolded the camp.

The fire died to glowing embers. The sound of snoring and the wind were the only noises upon the night air.

Robert sat with his back to the camp. The cart to his right side and the Loch before him. Silhouettes of the mountains could be seen in the distance and somewhere a hawk cried out before diving for it's prey. Robert heard not the footsteps behind him, nor did he see the flash of moonlight on the blade before it was driven into his back. A large hand covered his mouth to stifle the scream he tried to let out. Then nothing but darkness.

Roberts body lay lifeless in the heather. Two knights busied themselves filling saddle bags with the treasures from within the cart as the other kept watch over the sleeping occupants of the camp. Without a sound the Three rogue Knights led their horses away until they were out of sight of the camp, and with haste they rode West.

The cold chilly morning wind washed over William. He stood up and wrapped his cloak tight around him. Spying a small copse of trees away from the camp he set off to relieve himself. William breathed in. He tasted a familiar flavour. He sniffed the air once again and was greeted by a similar smell. One he had endured for many years. The smell of death.

He finished his business and drew his sword.
Glancing around the camp he noticed nothing unusual at
first. Then his gaze was drawn to the cart. Something was
different. The cloth cover had been partially removed and
it looked emptier.

"Get up we have been betrayed!" he shouted at the
camp. Soon all the Knights were stood on their feet as
William surveyed the area around the cart. It was then he
saw the body of his friend. Rushing over to the spot
Robert had fallen, William dropped to his knees.

He held the old man close to him and prayed.
Without being asked several of the knights set to and dug
a shallow grave for their fallen comrade. The burial was
short but respectful. "Do we go after them?" asked
Squire John.

He wanted revenge for the death of Robert. He too,
had become fond of the old man. William shook his
head. "No they are desperate men, I understand why they
did what they did, with France and England being
enemies of the Templar we must do what we can to
survive" he said mounting the cart.

Soon the party was on it's way. John now joined
William sat on the cart containing the rest of the treasures
that the betrayers could not carry. his horse tethered to
the rear they galloped along at a steady pace their hearts

heavy at the loss of a friend. Mountains led into deep forests. The knights were now more wary.

Despite most of the Scottish clans being in Ireland with The Bruce, tinkers still operated in some areas of the Highlands. The Journey toward Inverness was uneventful. William and John did not talk much. Both men mourned for Robert.

Neither shed a tear for fear of looking weak, despite their hearts being broken. "William, there is a castle to the East, perhaps we can find shelter there for tonight?" said Jauferre riding up to the cart and pointing toward a distant light. "Yes" replied William. "The men are weary and moral is low" he said looking around at the remaining knights.

Cawdor castle was a new construction rebuilt Ten years previous. It's predecessor had been sacked by The Bruce when it fell into English hands. Now new stone, painted white, stood in place of the crumbling masonry. William shouted up to the guard on the battlements. "My friend, I am but a humble Templar requesting shelter for myself and my brothers".

The guard turned to one of his colleagues and moments later the small drawbridge lowered allowing them access to the courtyard. "Good day to you sir, I am William, Third Thane of Cawdor" said an elderly gent stepping out of the keep. "sir, I am William Lyvett of Newlands I request lodgings for myself and my fellow knights if that be possible?" he asked politely.

"Ah Templar's eh, I heard you had all been captured?" said the Thane. "Not all sir" said Jauferre stepping forward. "I am Jauferre De St Clair of Caithness" he said holding his hand out and shaking the Thanes. "It is but a pleasure sir" said the Thane with a smile. Safe within the walls of the castle the Templar knights relaxed and began to enjoy the company of the Thane and his men.

Dice were thrown, competitions took place, the winners gaining favour of the Thanes beautiful wife. Although the Templar were sworn to abstinence this did not stop them feeling the urges men feel. Though they did not break their vows, they would pray for forgiveness later and enjoyed the attention of the females of court.

Thane William sat at the head of his table. "so my friends what will you do once you have taken your cargo to it's destination?" he asked throwing a bone to one of the large Irish wolfhounds who dived on it like an owl to a field mouse.

"I must confess I had not given it much thought" replied William interested by the question. What would he do once his quest was complete? He had no home to go back to and was an outlaw in his own country along with the other knights. "worry yourselves not with such thoughts" said Jauferre with a smile on his weathered face.

"you are most welcome to stay at my home for as long as you wish, my castle is your castle," he said placing a hand on Williams arm. "Thank you Jauferre I shall only stay as long as it takes to find my feet once more" replied William. "so how long will it take you to ride to St Clair castle?" asked the Thane. "We estimate another day or two's ride" replied Jauferre.

"Would going by sea not be quicker?" asked the Thane curiously. "Of course" replied William. "However we do not have a ship" he added. The Thane contemplated momentarily. " I may be able to help you there" he smiled.

The terrible stench of fish filled the Knights Templar's nostrils as they rode onto the harbour the next morning. With them rode the Thane William. He dismounted his horse and entered a small hut nearby. Returning moments later with a red faced over weight gent.

"This is Dougal my brother in law" he said introducing William and the knights to the man. "He is captain of the good ship 'Trebaruna'" he continued pointing to a large sea fairing vessel moored One Hundred yards downstream. "He will take you to Wick harbour safely and will more than halve the journey time" he finished with a smile.

The sea's around the North East Highlands were rough at the best of times. Soon man and horse found themselves being tossed around by the waves. They tethered themselves and the horses with ropes tightly to the mast so as not to be washed overboard. The knights themselves were seasoned sailors and none felt the sickness of the sea, save Squire John who spent the journey looking like the Green man of the woods and emptying his stomach contents over the port side.

As they sailed along, the harbour of Wick came in to sight. So too did a small armada of ships moored just off the coast. "Are those English ships?" called out William to the Captain. "Nay, here, take a look" replied the Captain handing over a spyglass .

William held the spyglass up to his eye and peered through the lens. What he saw made him gasp and let out a joyful yell. "What is it" asked John rushing to his side. "Templar ships" William smiled. "It seems more of our brethren escaped the clutches of the Kings" he said to Jauferre who had also joined them.

Jauferre took the eye glass from him and looked through it himself. "There must be Eight Hundred vessels" he said in awe. "May I take a look" asked Stefan joining the group. He smiled as he recognised several of the ships. "Those are the ships myself and my brother set sail with" he said with a grin.

It was a short ride to St Clair castle from the harbour at Wick and as they approached they were met with the sight of a small city made of canvas tents. Almost a Thousand knights busied themselves with every day tasks and training. The small group of Templar now led by Jauferre De St Clair rode through the camp. They were greeted by their brethren as they passed the tents. Stefan and David recognised a few of them. Knights who had stood and fought side by side with them in many a battle.

Jauferre ordered the company of knights to go and find somewhere to bed down and he, William and Squire John rode onward to the castle. The large English Oak gate opened as the riders approached and a beautiful red haired woman came running out.

"Jauferre, oh Jauferre I was so worried about you I thought you had been arrested along with the other Templar." she shouted running up to Jauferre and hugging him as he climbed down off his horse. "Malvina it is good to see you my sister" smiled Jauferre hugging her tightly. "Come Jauferre, Harold will be so excited to see you". She glanced at William and John. "Of course your friends must join us." She smiled, blushing slightly at the rugged yet handsome young squire.

Inside the dark castle, sat astride a stone chair, was a man in around Forty Years of age. From first glance one could be forgiven for mistaking him for a normal man, his long red hair flowing down over his shoulders. At closer inspection the disfigurement of the man's features could be deemed startling to some. William did not recoil in fear as most men when introduced to Henry.

He knelt in front of the man and bowed in respect. John followed suit although inside he was silently repulsed by the protruding jaw and lost cheek bones amongst what must have been flesh at one time. Jauferre hugged his brother who giggled like a new born baby relishing in his families love.

Malvina joined them carrying a jug of wine and some food. They all sat and ate in relative silence. Happy to not have to run or fight any more. They were safe in the solitude of St Clair castle and an army of Templar's guarding them outside. Days passed and the Templar became complacent with their situation. The treasure was safely hidden in the castles cellar and the remaining knights of the order settled into a life of peace.

5 THE SANCTUARY

Years passed.

Time and age caught up as it does with all men. One by One the Templar's grew old and passed away. Only William and the current Laird Sinclair, George, Second son of Jauferre and his younger brother Alexander remained at the castle along with the servants. George and Alexander's mother had died giving birth to Alexander and the young boy was lucky to have survived himself. When Jauferre died also Ten years later it was left to William and one of the maids to raise the children.

William now an old man himself hobbled into the great hall. "George my young friend I am not long for this world." He stammered as he laid a frail hand on the strong young man's shoulder. George turned from staring out of the window and smiled.

"William my old friend, my father would have been proud to see how well you have taught me. And when you are gone I shall build you a shrine to mark your resting place, A shrine worthy of the warrior you once were". William shook his head. "NO!" he scalded. "you must never mark where we once were." George shuddered at the tone of William's voice.

Even at Twenty years old the sound of the old man shouting made him wince with fear. "I am sorry" said

William sensing the fear in George. "There is something of importance I must burden you, and you alone with." He seated himself on the window ledge beside George. William began to reel off the story of his past and the treasures which lay beneath the castle. George's eyes lit up at the mention of the treasures. "May I see them?" he asked excitedly standing up.

William pulled him back to the ledge. "You may, however I must finish the tale first." William smiled at the enthusiastic youth. "The treasure is not safe here" he continued. "When I pass you must remove it all and take it high up into the mountains.

There you must find the most discrete location and leave no clues as to where it lays". George lowered his head in thought. "I think I know of just the place" he began but was interrupted by William. "It must be a place no one else knows of" he said knowing that George was thinking of a somewhere he and his brother played.

"You will know it when you come across it" smiled William leaning on George to stand from the ledge. "It is a beautiful day why not go hunting my young friend, enjoy the sun while it shines and the breeze upon your skin for one day you may crave such a thing".

The day passed and the night fell bringing with it eternal peace for William. His days were now gone and as George knelt beside the great Knight's bed he made a vow to keep his promise and deliver the treasure to a safe haven.

In William's hand was a large iron key and a note which read. *"guard it well until Sanctuary is found."* George took the key and made his way to the cells.

The stairs were dank and slippery and even the flames of the torch he held did not relieve much of the darkness. In George's youth no one would set foot in the dungeons for fear of ghosts. Tales told to them by his father and William, obviously to keep the treasure from being discovered.

He stepped cautiously along the long stone corridor the shadows of Iron bars from each empty cell leapt at him vigorously as he passed. He imagined the screams of long gone prisoners who once occupied the tight, rank smelling holes. A large oak door stood in front of him guarding the corridor. Removing the key he turned it in the lock and with a loud groan the door opened.

George shielded his eyes as the torchlight illuminated the gold and silver within the small room. He dropped to his knees at the sight of such riches, then gathering his senses he made plans to remove the items. To avoid suspicion from any other in the castle he would do the task each night. Long after the moon had risen he crept down into the dungeons and brought bag after bag of the treasures to the stables where he hid them behind the large bails of hay.

After three nights of back breaking work he picked up the final bag and closed the oak door behind him. George headed out of the castle gates with a large cart. He took a glance back and remembered the words William had spoken *"you will know it when you come across it"*.

With this in mind he rode into the cold night. A fog rolled in from the sea like a dragons breath. Engulfing George and the treasure as he travelled through the dark. George's footing slipped on the damp heather as he stumbled along the pass.

Seven Days and Nights passed and deeper into the Highland wilderness did he clamber. As he reached the summit of a small outreach of rocks he spotted a small brook. He traced the outline. Following it first West, toward a large loch. Then East and up toward the mountainous wilderness. Perched on the banks of the brook was a small crofters cottage. The roof no longer protected the interior from the elements but it would keep the wind out for a while and provide some shelter.

Building a small fire George sat down and ate. He leant against the crumbling stone walls and reached into his sporran removing a silver pendant on a chain. He let the chain spin in his fingertips the firelight danced off the image of a horse and two riders.

The seal of the Templar given to him when he was but a child by his father. George fastened the talisman around his neck and let it rest. The metal was cold against his damp skin. Even the flickering flames did not warm him through.

Rest did not last long for George and before the light rose once more he set off, following the water upstream. He held the reigns of the carthorse firmly. The terrain was tough for them both.

Large crops of moss and fern grew as he pulled himself and the horse up the hill side. He stopped in his tracks and eyed the stream cautiously. Following the flow upwards, only yards ahead of him, the entrance to a cavern was slightly obscured by fast running water and vegetation. George tied the horse to a nearby rock. He ventured forward through the sheet of ice cold water, stopping momentarily to take a drink before stepping into the darkness.

Reaching into the large bag he had retrieved from the cart, he pulled out a wooden torch. George struck the blade of his Sgian-Dubh against a rock sending sparks into the dry grass he held. Soon he had his torch lit and he could see his surroundings.

Water droplets caressed the walls of the cavern which seemed to disappear into blackness before him. The depths of the cave were quite a spectacular vision. He must have walked almost a mile and deep into the underbelly of the mountain. A glow of crystals embedded within the walls, floors and ceiling illuminated the cathedral cavern. "yes" he thought to himself, "this is it, this is the safe haven William spoke of."

He turned around and returned to the surface to find the horse still tethered and his load undisturbed. Slowly he began the tedious job of carrying his cargo down into the cave. Once all the treasures were laid safely amongst the crystals he vowed to stay and guard them until his last breath.

6 THE CURSE

Many would hear the tales of the Templar and the mysterious disappearance of the treasures.

Just like the ripples of time, the stories were told and added to, until before long the truth was lost amongst the bedtime tales of brave knights.

What was not told was that before George left the castle of St Clair he told one other of the treasure. His younger brother being still not of age when George left seemed a trustworthy ally in keeping the secret. Unbeknown to George the young Alexander followed him into the darkness that night.

For Seven Days, and Seven nights, Alexander stalked his kin like a hunter stalking a stag. Then he sat hidden amongst the heather watching as George descended and ascended from the cave. Night fell and darkness engulfed the land. Alexander crept inside the cavern and made his way to the depths below.

He stopped and marvelled at the vast treasure before him. Ducking into the shadows he held his breath as his brother busied himself with the fire and roasting a rabbit he had caught. Alexander eyed him cautiously, then glanced back toward the treasure. Slowly he crept. The shadows hid him well and it was too late by the time

George realised there was someone behind him. The large axe slammed down against George's skull. A scattering of warm liquid erupted over Alexander as his weapon struck it's target.

George fell to the ground. He turned his head and saw his brother staring at him. George muttered a curse beneath his last breath. Then, he was gone, only his corpse remained. Realisation hit home as Alexander stood staring at the blood on his hands and the lifeless corpse at his feet.

He sobbed softly at first, then began to wail like a banshee. Dropping to his knees he picked his brother up into his arms. The life had left George and only the vessel which once carried his soul remained now draped in the young boy's arms. The sight of the treasure had driven him to madness, to murder.

Winter came and left. Alexander remained living, if living is what it was, in the cavern. His brothers rotting corpse the only company seated on a roughly carved throne. A diet of rabbit, rat and the odd fish kept Alexander healthy in body only. His mind was as rotten as the flesh dripping from Georges corpse.

Many years passed by and no one came close to the cavern. Those few who did were scared off by the ramblings of a mad man screaming from the top of the waterfall.

As the years passed the area became known as Bedlamite falls and few who valued their lives ventured there. One such person who did not value his life was a young sheep herder. Donald Ross of the Clan Ross.

He was the only son of Charles Ross one of the Five elders. At aged Sixteen, despite his father being an important man, he loved to spend time in the hills watching over the sheep.

The Spring equinox was upon the Country and throughout the mountains and glens. The herders were busy with lambing season. Gangly legged clumsy animals were born and soon the bleating of new born lambs rang through the glens.

Donald was tending to the herd which had wandered down to the great Loch at the base of the mountain. As he counted the sheep and lambs he realised there was a new lamb missing from the flock. He knew he must find it. If wolves had taken it there must be some trace.

Looking around his gaze followed the inlet of the loch upstream. He spotted a little white cloud running up the hill. "Ah there you are you wee tinker!" he exclaimed taking off after the lamb. His feet were nimble on the heather clad ground as he bounded up the hill. The lamb was only feet away from him as he reached the top.

"C'mere ya wee beggar." He lurched forward and caught the lamb between his arms. Giving a disgruntled bleat the animal settled itself knowing that Donald meant it no harm.

Donald sat on a nearby rock to catch his breath and take in the view as he often liked to do. Glancing around something caught his eye amongst a large outcrop of rocks. He stood to get a better view.

Donald lowered the lamb carefully to the ground and shooting it a disapproving look as it sped off toward the flock below, he stepped across the shallow brook. The large boulders were jagged and looked to have been placed there by something not of this world.

Like the teeth of a whale protruding upward, a large crevice between them held an ugly secret. Donald leant over to look between the rocks. There lay the madman.

Alexander's arms were twisted up behind his back. Bones protruding from his legs, the blood long since drained and his skin was grey from decomposition.

Reaching down, Donald grasped the rags hanging off the body. He pulled with all his strength. With a lot of huffing and swearing eventually Alexander's corpse lay at Donald's feet. Knowing it was the right thing to do he began to gather rocks to build a cairn and give the man a proper burial.

Soon he had enough to begin and dragged the body to a more suitable location on a small plateau overlooking the loch. As he started to place the rocks around Alexander he noticed a small silver chain hanging out of the dead man's pocket. Removing this he ran his fingertips over the Templar seal at the end. Not knowing what the seal was, it seemed a shame to bury such a beautiful trinket and so he placed it in his own pocket before finishing the cairn.

That evening as he sat beside the fire with his father he relayed the days events. "Let me see this trinket you found" said his father leaning over and holding his hand out. Donald let the seal drop into the old man's weathered hands. Charles Ross gasped as he saw the horse and two riders. "Do you know what you have here my son." Donald shook his head. "No father I felt it too beautiful to bury beneath a cairn, I hope I did not do wrong." He winced expecting a slap from his father. It never came.

"This my son, is the seal of the greatest order of knights to have ever lived. This is the seal of the Knights of the temple of Solomon." Charles moved his chair closer to the fire to view the stunning workmanship of the item. As the flames lit up his bright red hair, Charles told his son the story of the Templar.

Even though only Forty years had passed since the disappearance of George and Alexander, the story was beginning to gather interest from many people far and wide. "And so Donald, the man you buried must have been one of the last Templar knights. Who knows, perhaps he was even the guardian of the treasure the stories speak of." laughed Charles.

Though he knew much of the story to be true, there were also many "folk tales" giving explanations and theories as to what happened to the treasure. "In the morning you can show me the cairn you built. But now it is time for rest. Go on get" he smiled clipping Donald around the ear softly. Donald smiled at his father and bid him goodnight.

Horses galloped across the glen and stopped by the hillside, The cold water of Bedlamite falls sprayed over the two riders as they dismounted. "This way father" said Donald excitedly clambering up the hillside. Charles followed his son to the top of the falls. There, a large cairn of stones stood proudly. "That is a fine cairn indeed Donald. You have done the knight proud." He smiled patting his son on the shoulder.

As they sat on a large boulder eating their lunch the father and son looked out across the glen. There had been relative peace among the clans for years and the tranquillity of the highlands was enough to quieten the hottest of mouths. Crickets chirped. Birds sang. The day passed by and both Father and Son felt at peace with the world around them as they rode home.

Nine years more came and passed. On Donald's
Twenty Fifth day since his birth he was given a small
plot of land by the river only half a mile from Bedlamite
falls. Here, with his new bride Isla, Donald built a
farmstead where he raised a few cattle and sheep and
worked the land beside the river.

He travelled to the city one day and returned with a
small cross bred dog. "Oh Donald what have ya brought
that mutt home with you for" said Isla who couldn't help
but smile at the black dog's cute features and single white
spot over his eye. "I guess we will have to call you
patch" she said ruffling the dogs ears and kissing her
husband on the cheek. "Now outside with ya" she said
shuffling both Donald and the pup into the yard. "Supper
will be ready in an hour" she shouted through the open
doorway. "Take this and catch me a fish my love" she
added handing the fishing pole through the door to
Donald.

Suicidal tiny insects hovered above the fast flowing
water. Just waiting to become a tasty treat for a topping
salmon. As did the long wriggly worm on Donald's hook.
The fish were not biting this warm summers eve and so
after a disappointing hour Donald and Patch returned
home to a meal of vegetable stew and corn bread. "He
can wait outside" said Isla as the pair trundled through
the door. "Sorry my friend, the boss has spoken" smiled

Donald picking the dog up and carrying him back outside. He tethered him to a nearby post, patted his head and left Patch to scratch the days fleas from his fur.

Darkness fell and the land became still around the farm. Isla lay in Donald's arms by the fire. Neither spoke, they just relished one another's company. The silence was broken by a yapping from outside. "Perhaps we should let him in for the night" said Donald. "After all he is still a pup." He smiled at his wife knowing she couldn't resist his deep brown eyes and mischievous grin. "Just for tonight" she said as Donald got up and left the cottage.

"PATCH! Here boy." Donald shouted into the dark. There was no sound. The barking had ceased. "Patch, where are ye" Donald called once more.

He then noticed the rope which he had tethered to the dog had been chewed through. "Dam it" he swore. "Isla! Isla that dam dog has run off" he called to his wife. "It's too dark to try and find him now" said Isla appearing at the door. "Come to bed, and in the morning we will both go look for him." Donald stared into the darkness. "Aye my love" he agreed returning to the cottage. They settled down for the night.

The cockerel screeched it's morning alarm. The sun rose, casting eerie shadows and reflections over the loch. Isla was already awake and busying herself preparing breakfast when Donald got out of his bed. He stepped up behind her, and slipping his strong arms around her slender waist he leant over and kissed her neck gently. Shudders ran through her body.

She turned and kissed him passionately. "Good morning my love" she smiled.

Once breakfast was eaten and the animals fed the couple headed out to look for Patch. It was a hot day so Isla carried a deerskin bottle of water slung over her shoulder. Donald carried a long staff to help navigate any rough terrain and as they walked they whistled and called the dog's name. "I hope we find him" said Isla as they reached the top of a hill.

"Aye lass, me too" replied Donald. "We shall rest here for a while" he continued seeing that his wife was sweating. "yes" she agreed before suddenly collapsing into his arms. "Isla, my love, wake up." The words echoed around in her head like the cries of an eagle. Slowly she opened her eyes.

"D..Donald what happened?" she asked shakily. "You fainted my love. Here drink" he said holding her head up and tilting the deer hide bottle toward her lips. She soon began to feel better and sat upright.

Leaning against her husband's torso she pulled his arms around her not because she was cold but because she felt something special was happening inside her. She would not tell Donald until she was certain though.

As they sat embraced among the heather. The wind which blew softly, carried with it a faint sound. "Did you hear that?" asked Donald. Isla shook her head. The wind blew once more and surfing amongst it was a soft barking noise. "It's Patch!" exclaimed Donald as he helped Isla up from the ground. "Come on this way."

He set off toward the barking which grew louder, until all of a sudden it stopped. All that was left was the roar of Bedlamite falls cascading down the rocks ahead of them. "Where did he go?" asked Isla looking around at the foliage and jagged rocks. "I don't know. He was here, I know he was" replied Donald confused. He clambered down to a platform where the falls levelled before the water hurtled down into the brook below.

"Here. This way" he said helping his wife down and pointing to an opening behind the falls. "He must have gone in the madman's cave" said Isla knowing of the stories. "Be careful Donald" she said worriedly.

Donald grinned at his wife. "Tis OK my love. Come we will go together and when we find that mutt he's in big trouble." He took Isla's hand and led her into the darkness "it's too dark" she sobbed. "What was that!" shrieked Isla. Her foot caught against something hard.

Something which made a dull thud as she kicked it. Donald lent down and felt the ground. Moving his hand slowly he felt what Isla had kicked. As he ran his hand up the item he realised with relief that it was made of wood. Reaching the end of the item he felt soft material.

"It's a torch!" he exclaimed lifting it up. He removed his Dirk and struck the blade against the cave wall. Sparks danced their way onto the material of the torch. The flame casting a glow around the cave. Isla felt more comfortable now they had a light source. Though she still held her husband's hand tightly she was beginning to enjoy the adventure.

They descended through long winding tunnels. A soft glow ahead of them stopped the couple in their tracks. "Is there someone in there?" Isla asked. "I don't know" said Donald. "It doesn't look like normal firelight to me" he continued. "Wait here" he said handing the torch to Isla and stepping cautiously toward the glow. There was the sound of yapping and Donald called out. "Patch you wee tinker, there you are."

Isla came around the corner and saw her husband being molested by the young dog's tongue. It was the cavern she stood in however, which left her speechless and in awe. Donald did not lift his head and so the treasures in front of him were not visible. Nor did he hear Isla sneak up behind him. A blade tight in her hand. Her eyes were black and soulless. She raised the blade and struck her husband in the back several times. He fell forward in a pool of blood and Isla stared at the blade in her hand.

She then looked down at Donald. She dropped to her knees, calling out his name. Tears blinded her as she battled with the guilt of what she had just done. The thought of killing her husband overwhelmed her and at first, without hesitation, she raised the blade once more. The tip aimed at her heart.

She was about to plunge it deep into her chest when she felt a sharp pain in her stomach. Dropping the blade to the floor she doubled over in pain. As it subsided she knew for certain that she carried Donald's child inside her.

She could take her husband's life and her own but not that of an innocent. Gathering her thoughts she dragged Donald deeper into the cavern. Hiding his body behind the large pile of gold and jewels, there his corpse would stay and rot, until only a pile of bones remained.

Isla picked up the dog and returned home. People never visited Isla and so there was none to ask any questions about her husband. She would lie and tell them he went out hunting and never returned if anyone wandered that way.

Spring and summer came and went. Winter arrived bringing with it the cold and snow. Isla gave birth to a healthy boy and named him Charles Donald after his father and Grandfather. Her mind had begun to dissolve and though she coped with bringing the child up within Six years her mind was almost gone. Only a shell remained.

Sat upon the porch overlooking the brook. Her eyes stared deep into the darkness as though waiting for something, or someone. Perhaps the return of her husband.

young Charles had learnt to grow up quickly and at Six years of age he could cook, clean, hunt and prepare a deer or fish as well as any older boy. He returned from fishing. Four large salmon balanced in his arms. "Fish for tea mother." He smiled dropping them on the porch beside his parent. Isla did not acknowledge the boy she just stared into the night.

Three more years went by. More and more withdrawn Isla became. Finally she gave in. The guilt and shame had built up inside her it was too much to bare. Without saying goodbye to her son she walked up to the top of Bedlamite Falls. She eyed the cave cautiously. Turning her back to the cave she threw herself over the edge and onto the rocks laying in the brook fifty feet below.

The impact killed her instantly and her distorted body flowed downstream into the loch. It would be many months before he found her and by then she was almost unrecognisable. Charles had spent every day searching for her, and as he saw her corpse in the water, he collapsed to the ground sobbing.

Charles knew he couldn't stay at the farm. He had no money. No food. The crops he had planted had died before he could harvest them. Rummaging through the draws of his fathers cabinet he found the silver amulet depicting the knights Templar.

Placing it into his pocket he grabbed as much as he could carry and set off over the mountain.

Heading South he followed an old sheep herders track. It was cold and boggy as he made his way down to the glen below. He slipped on a wet rock. Flailing and grappling at the air trying to get a hold of something secure to stop him falling, he went face first into the bog. His feet were sore and bleeding. Dirt covered his face and torso as he stumbled into the small village of Cannich.

The village stood several miles South of his home. A young woman saw him hobbling down the street and ran out to him. "Oh my poor wee bairn, come, come inside let's get you cleaned up, tell me what happened to you?" she asked hustling the boy into her small house. The fire burned warmly as Charles sat beside it. His face and wounds now clean, he hungrily ate the bread and cheese the woman had given him.

Marianne McCleod was a beautiful young woman with long blonde hair and deep blue eyes. Many a boy in the village wished to court her but Marianne was not interested in any of them. Charles had told Marianne of his mother and the story she had told him of how his father had disappeared while hunting.

Tears flowed down his face as he relayed how Isla had walked out, and how he found her body in the loch. Marianne wiped a tear from her own eye and handed a handkerchief to William who took it with a thank you. He wiped his own eyes and blew his nose then offered it back.

Marianne smiled. "No you keep it" she said not wanting the snot filled rag back. "You must stay here" she insisted. "I will look after you." She ruffled the boys hair and Charles felt himself blushing crimson from her touch.

Only Eight years in age separated Charles and Marianne and through the years the boy grew into a handsome young man. Feelings stirred between them both and as his Eighteenth birthday came and passed as often happens in life, the two became lovers.

They were married late that summer and before long were expecting the first of what was to become a very large family. Charles put behind him the horrors of his childhood and grew into a respectable member of the community.

Winters and summers came and went as did the lives of Charles and Marianne. Their belongings handed down to their kin, and their kin after them. Throughout the centuries the seal of the Templar's was handed down from father to first born son. None knowing it's significance or history.

The summer of 1540 was the hottest on record. So hot, it dried up many small lochs and streams. One of these was Bedlamite falls. The source of the brook now depleted and only sand remained to show where once fresh water flowed. The remote land around the falls, and the Ross farmstead, were said to be dangerous. Timothy Pont , map maker, was one of the few men to venture so far North. To many the Highlands were a place of death and despair.

7 THE AGE OF DISCOVERY

London 1885. The age of industry and discovery.

There were many men whom had turned their interests to mechanics or engineering. Then there were those academics who wished to discover more of the past.

Sir James Mc McGregor was a doctorate of history. Graduating from Cambridge, his field of interest was medieval history. He sat in his dark oak walled study.

One wall was lined with dusty books. A large map of North England and Scotland was nailed to the wooden panelling on the opposite wall. A large globe perched upon an ornate carved wooden stand adorned one corner of the study and a display cabinet with ancient artefacts safe behind the glass. James sat at his desk thumbing through some papers and maps scattered over the redwood surface.

Outside, the bustling streets of London choked with smog. People went about their business as usual. James glanced out of the window watching passers by. His hand laid upon his bearded chin as he pondered. There was a knock and Cathy the housemaid poked her curly head around the door.

"Master, there is a gentleman to see you" she said pushing the oak door open wide. "Who is it Cathy? I told you I was not to be disturbed" said James spinning on his heels angrily. The anger soon dispersed when he saw who was calling upon him.

"My dear Ernest what a pleasure it is to see you!" smiled James extending a hand to his old friend and tutor. Ernest took it with a grin upon his face, "To what do we owe this pleasure?" asked James knowing that Ernest was a busy man.

"I have come to ask you to join me on an expedition of archaeological importance" said Ernest seating himself in James's desk chair. "And where would this expedition be?" asked James pouring himself and his friend a drink. "I have heard tale of a lost farmstead with connections to the Templar Knights" Replied Ernest taking the drink and downing it in one go.

He passed the glass back for a refill and waved his hand as James poured. He held his hand up, motioning for James to stop pouring and reached for the glass.

"So why come to me?" asked James sipping his own drink. "I believe, this may be of interest to you" said Ernest reaching into his pocket he removed a small wooden box and slid it across the desk. James picked up the curiosity. Eyeing it with contempt, he lifted the lid and was greeted with a silver chain.

Tethered to the end of the finely crafted links was a round disc with a faded image of a single horse and two riders. "Is this real?" he asked fingering the talisman with care. "yes my friend, it has been dated to 1292 it is indeed an original seal" smiled Ernest. "Where did you get this from?" enquired James placing it back into the box and handing it back to Ernest. "it came to me along with the journal of the late William Ross of Stirling" he replied.

The next week was taken up with James busying himself in preparation for the long journey North. Despite him being of Scots decent himself, he had never even stepped foot North of Sheffield. The day came when Ernest and his team of Archaeologists arrived to pick James up.

He clambered up into the carriage as the driver struggled to find space for his luggage. "Good day gentlemen" said James removing his hat and squeezing onto the seat beside Ernest. "Let me introduce you to my colleagues who will be accompanying us on this trip" said Ernest gesturing to the two men in front of them.

"This, is Dr Howard Johnson, and Christopher, Howard's son." James nodded his head and greeted the two men who sat quietly, almost as if they were disgusted by James's presence. "Have you ever travelled by train before?" aske Ernest as they arrived at the station.

Thick black smoke erupted as the train roared to a standstill and the passengers boarded. "No this is the first time" said James grabbing his bags and dragging them onto the train. The compartment he would be sharing with Ernest was comfy in comparison to the coach and horses he was used to. He soon settled into his seat as the train pulled out of the station.

The journey North was a pleasant one. The scenery was breathtaking. James and Ernest talked most of the journey until both felt too tired and drifted to sleep.

They were awoken by Howard and Christopher just as they arrived at Edinburgh station. from here they would have to hire horses and ride the rest of the way up toward the Highlands.

Stirling castle loomed high upon its rock perch. Standing proudly overlooking the City below. It's white walls gleaming in the afternoon sun. The horse and carriage Ernest had hired wasn't built well and it shook, groaned and creaked at every crevice and crack in the roads and tracks. The four occupants held on for dear life as they rumbled into the City. "Woaaah!" called the driver to his horse. The dapple grey mare slowed to a halt outside a tavern.

"Stirling, Everyone out!" the driver shouted through the open window of the carriage. Inside the tavern was much as James had expected. Ancient oak beams adorned the ceiling. The walls painted chalk white held decorations of claymores and other weaponry. The barkeep eyed the four men as they struggled inside with their belongings. "what will it be?" asked the barman. "We require rooms and food please barkeep" said Ernest placing Five Guineas on the bar.

"Right away sir" smiled the barman sweeping up the coins in his hand. "My name is Harold and anything you need I'm your man" he said leaving the bar. "This way" he beckoned. Once they had settled into their rooms the four men met downstairs in the tap room to discuss their next steps.

Pine logs burned in the fireplace as the companions sipped pints of ale, Ernest told them the information he had discovered about the pendant.

"As I told you in London. The pendant was left to me by my good friend William Ross. It was a long time since we last met so as you may imagine it was a surprise to receive the item."

Ernest coughed to clear his throat and took a drink. He lifted his Meerschaum pipe to his lips and lit it, sucking in the tobacco before letting it drift out his mouth and upward toward the ceiling. He pushed his glasses up to the bridge of his nose and continued.

"The Templar seal was given only to the knights of the highest rank. For a man of low birth, such as William to come into possession of such a thing can mean it was either found or came to him by ill gains". No one spoke as Ernest explained that he knew William to be a noble man so the latter was not even in the equation. It was now that James spoke up.

"What if it was left to him by a member of his family?" he asked. "Ah yes, indeed that may also be the case. He had no sons or daughters. He did have a sister who also lived in these parts, Rosemary I believe her name is." He broke off into a trail of thought only brought back by James shaking his arm. "Ernest, Ernest!" James called. "Yes? Oh my I must have drifted off there. You may be correct James. We must find Rosemary" said Ernest excitedly. "Tomorrow we will begin our search" said James raising his glass in a toast.

With this new plan in action the Archaeology expedition was put on hold for a few days. The four men travelled the length and breadth of the City asking about Rosemary Ross. James was the first one back to the tavern on the third day of their search, closely followed by Christopher and his father. "Have you seen Ernest?" asked Howard handing James a mug of ale. "Thank you. No not since this morning. Did you have any luck?" he replied taking the mug and setting it down on the table.

Ernest arrived, not giving Howard a chance to reply. He was sweating as though he had been running. "I-I've found her" he gasped. "she's at Cowane's hospital. I spoke to her." He sat down and motioned to the barman to bring him a drink.

"Tell us what did she say?" asked Christopher. Howard placed a hand on his sons shoulder. "Let the man rest Christopher" he said. "My apologies sir" added Howard taking a gulp of his drink. "No apology is required" Ernest said graciously.

"Rosemary was very forthcoming with information on her family" began Ernest as he took the drink from Harold who had just appeared behind him. He nodded his thanks to the barkeep and continued. "It seems we may be heading to the wrong place. Rosemary was adamant that her family was from a small village named Cannich a few miles South of our original destination".

The rain lashed at the window pain of the Golden Fleece tavern. A single candle burned inside one of the rooms. Ernest sat in his night gown. His glasses perched on the edge of his nose and a bundle of papers on his knees and by his side scattered over the bed.

He removed a small parchment from a leather case and unrolled it carefully. Placing a shoe on one end of the parchment he lent down and studied the map intently. he traced a line along the mountain tops with his fingers for several inches then stopped tapping his finger tip over a small area.

At breakfast the next day Ernest told his friends that he had found the village on an old map but the only way to get there would be by horse. No carriage would make it across terrain such as which lay ahead of them.

The stench of the stables was what one would expect. Horse manure, steaming and smelly, piled in the corner next to bales of hay. Ernest stood talking to the breeder explaining the distance and terrain they would be travelling.

The horse trader showed him four very fine looking stallions. All brown with black manes which would flow in the wind. "Yes these are fine looking beasts we will take them." The trader smiled knowing they would not be cheap and he could afford a decent meal for a change. Ernest also purchased two young pack horses to carry their luggage.

As they set off through the streets of Stirling, they looked a comical sight. They stopped only to stock up on food and other provisions for the Four day journey ahead. The rain was falling softly. Despite the sun shining. The four men rode across moorland and shallow bogs. They stopped at mid day for some food at a small village. The village of Callander which stood at the foot of Mount Uamh Bheag. They drank in the splendour of the mountains majesty towering above them.

The rain had begun to grow faster and by evening the four men rolled into the village of Killin resembling drowned mariners more than Archaeologists. They crossed the bridge over the falls of Dochart and found shelter in a nearby barn for the night.

The barn had obviously been abandoned for years and only remnants of the owners remained. The roof was in disrepair and droplets of water cascaded in showers through the holes. Much of the barn was still dry.

Christopher found a fireplace where he built a small fire to dry their clothes and warm them. luckily there was an abundance of dry timber available inside the building more than enough to see them through the storm raging outside.

The horses were restless. James stood and walked over to where they were tethered at the far end of the large building. "Steady there fella's" he whispered patting each horse one by one on the neck. As the wind howled its wolf song outside the horses began to calm and settle at his touch and voice.

Later that night the group were awoken suddenly. A crash of thunder so loud it was as if it had been sent by the God's themselves. The building shook frantically as streaks of lightning struck the walls. Bricks and timber began to fall. Clouds of dust erupted inside the building as three men struggled to escape the impending wreckage. "Where's James?" shouted Howard looking around. "he was right here" replied Ernest worriedly.

"He must be still inside. Wait here, I'll get him" shouted Christopher running back inside. It was almost pitch black inside save a few small fires set by the lightning.

Listening intently Christopher heard a quiet moaning from the rear of the building behind a heap of rubble.

"James, James, can you hear me!" he called scrambling over the debris. "I-I'm here" coughed James trying to raise his arm. He was pinned by an oak ceiling beam.

"The horses? Did they make it?" he shouted almost choking on the words. Christopher tried to see where the horses had been tethered but all that remained there was a pile of bricks and mortar. "No, I don't think they did, come on let's get you out of here" he replied heaving on the heavy beam. With a creak and a groan the beam shifted just enough for James to slide from beneath it. save for a few scratches and bruises he was unharmed. Together with Christopher they gathered what belongings they could find and stumbled out into the fresh air and rain.

Hearing the commotion, an old woman and her husband arrived at the scene. "Oh you poor dears. Come you must have something to eat and drink with us." she said taking Ernest by the arm and leading the men toward a small cottage by the loch. "It was only a matter of time before that old place came down" said the old man pouring beakers of whisky for his guests. "Here this is from our own distillery. It'll put hairs on ye chest" he smiled handing the drinks over.

"So what were ye doing in the old Kindale barn" asked the old man's wife. "We were bedding down for the night madam, and we thank you and your husband for your generous and kind hospitality" said Ernest sat by the fire. He explained their presence in the village and where they were heading. "you will need new horses" said the old man. "Aggie here will take you to the stables in the morning" he added as he and his wife left the men alone by the fire and headed to bed.

The morning brought with it dark brooding clouds but it was dry that at least they could be thankful for. "I'm afraid we only have Two old mares but you are welcome to them" said Aggie as she led the men to the stable. "Thank you Aggie, here please take this for your troubles and for the horses" said Howard handing the old woman a handful of coins.

"Oh no I couldn't take that" she replied trying to give the money back. Howard insisted and so she pocketed the coins and bid them farewell. Four men could not ride Two horses. And so they walked. Using the old beasts to carry their belongings. They followed the trail through Glen Ogleand. On to **Kenmore** on the Western head of Loch Tay. Here they would rest once more.

The small village housed several Linen Mills. A few cottages where the workers lived, and a coaching Inn on the outskirts of town. Here the men settled in for the evening.

"Have ye been fishing on the loch?" asked the barkeep as they ordered drinks. "No it isn't something we normally partake in" replied James paying the man. "If ye like I could take ye out on my boat in the morning" offered the barman. James considered the offer, then accepted agreeing to meet the man at Six am in order to go out on the lake. The others declined preferring instead to enjoy the comfort of their beds after such a journey, a journey which by no means was at an end.

A low mist hung over the lake as the small vessel drifted across the water. "This be a good spot" said Alfred the barkeep dropping a heavy anchor into the cold water. He handed a rod to James.

After a few lessons casting with a fly, James seemed to be a natural and swung the rod back and forth with elegance and grace. The fly on the end of his line skimming across the surface of the loch. "Here we go!" shouted Alfred as he reeled in a nice sized trout.

Moments later James got a bite too. His rod bent double and he struggled to gain control. "Let her have some line Laddy" said Alfred reaching over and releasing the reel. The fish eventually tired itself and James, despite the burning in his arms, reeled her in.

"Well done Master James, that has to be a record sized salmon if ever I saw one" said Alfred leaning over and pulling the enormous Fifty pound fish on board. A few more hours, and a pile of fish of all sizes later, they moored up on the bank.

"Thank you Alfred that was very enjoyable and something I will not forget in a long time" said James rubbing his aching arm muscles. "Twas my pleasure master James and we shall have fish for breakfast before your journey ahead" smiled Alfred leaving James to enjoy the sunrise.

The aroma of the large baked salmon was beautiful as Alfred emerged from the kitchen, slices of Lemon laid on top of the fish, he served it up to the four men with a smile. "Won't you join us Alfred" pleaded James. "After all if it was not for you we would not be eating this fish" he added pulling a stool out for the man to sit down. Alfred could not refuse and soon they were enjoying the food and conversation.

It was around Ten AM when the group left the inn. They headed to the nearest stables and purchased Four fresh horses before carrying on their way North. If they were to reach Cannock before the week was through they must hurry thought Ernest as they rode across the rugged terrain.

The next few days passed without event and gradually they rode down the mountain side and into the village that Rosemary Ross had mentioned.

Cannock was itself a small place, with only a few cottages. Many of it's inhabitants had left during the great highland clearing, leaving only a few families.

There was no Inn and so the four men made a makeshift camp in the forest on the North side of the village. Christopher was no stranger to the wilds and soon had the tent erected and a fire burning. "I spent Three years in the army." he explained to James as they chatted and cooked food.

"So what are you doing with yourself now?" asked James as he stirred the pot of stew. "I am a student of medicine at the royal college," replied Christopher "Medical surgical procedures to be precise." he added passing a small bag of salt to James. "So why did you join this expedition?" asked James emptying a pinch of salt into the pot.

"My father and I never spent much time together and when Ernest mentioned about this place being reportedly a Templar farmstead, well I had to come" he smiled. Christopher had always had an interest in the order of Templar Knights. He had read books of their exploits in the holy lands and knew of the legends behind the treasures.

The next day was spent interrogating the locals. One elderly woman remembered the Ross family. She recalled that the original farmstead was located somewhere by the brook near Loch a' Mhuilidh on the far side of the mountain, but could not remember the exact location. None of the residents could tell them more and so they headed across the mountain and down into the glen of Ardchuilk.

The sky was blue and the sun sparkled on the surface of the loch as they crossed the ford. Ahead of them stood a roofless ruin. At last they had found it. James, Christopher and Howard busied themselves erecting the large heavy canvas tent as a permanent base. Ernest wandered around the ruins. Examining and running his hands over the old stone as though expecting them to speak to him with tales of old. The excavations began slowly and all that was found were broken pots and animal bones during the first days.

On the seventh day something exciting was discovered.

As James scraped away between two large stone bricks a small hole appeared. He removed the dirt gently with his wooden trowel and brush revealing a larger hole ten inches wide. Peering inside he could not see much at first. Then something caught his eye buried beneath more loose dirt. Something shiny.

He reached inside and rummaged about cautiously. His hand found the object. Softly he pulled and the item shifted with ease. Removing it from the hole, he realized it was a leather journal with a brass buckle fastening the pages shut.

How old it was he could not tell but he knew he must show the others straight away. James rushed into the tent where Ernest, Howard and Christopher were enjoying a well earned break.

"Ernest, Ernest, look what I found buried beneath the wall of the house" he called out. He stumbled slightly. His foot slipping on a muddy patch at the tent doorway almost dropping the journal. "Oh my," he muttered straightening himself "here take a look at this." he said as he handed the book to Ernest.

With much care Ernest opened the delicate buckle afraid that the pages may fall apart. The relic was well preserved and dated to around the 1400's. Many of the pages were unrecognisable. And Ernest struggled to decipher what was written. "It seems to be a diary of sorts. Written in old Gaelic." he said examining the writing with his magnifying glass.

The expression on his face changed from curiosity, to awe as he translated the words.

"*I killed him. I can not bare what I did to my love and to the wee bairn inside me.*"

He coughed, clearing a lump from his throat he read on.

"*The wealth of what is secured there is too much for one person to withstand. I shall not visit Bedlamite any more.*"

Ernest looked puzzled "Bedlamite?" he muttered loudly. "A Bedlamite is a madman" he added matter of factly and buried his nose back into the ancient pages continuing to read out loud.

"*Soon my time will end. When Charles is old enough to look after himself, I shall end this torment and none shall know where the cursed treasure lays.*"

Ernest shook his head "no this can not be" he exclaimed excitedly. "My friends. I believe this journal is that of Isla Ross. I heard tales of the madwoman of Ardchuilk, but thought them only folklore" he said finally composing himself.

"And the treasure she speaks of?" asked Howard. "That my friend, I am unsure. There is some clue in Bedlamite you can be sure of that" replied Ernest. "James get me my brown leather satchel please" he asked pointing to the bag in a corner.

James handed the bag to him and Ernest rummaged through, throwing pieces of paper around the tent as he searched.

"Ah here it is" he said smiling and rolling out a hand drawn map of the highlands. "This is the first known map of this area, made on the order of Robert The Bruce himself" said Ernest placing his magnifying glass on on edge to level the parchment out. He leant over and stared intently at the map making strange noises and running his fingers through his grey hair.

"Ah yes, here, look, Bedlamite falls" he pointed to a small drawing of a waterfall. "that's only half a mile or so away" said Christopher "let's go look now" he added grabbing his bag of tools. "Wait Christopher, I walked up that way yesterday, I saw no water fall" said Howard. "Perhaps you are mistaken Ernest" he said with a touch of guilt in his voice for questioning his friend.

"No no it was definitely there in Isla Ross's day" replied Ernest. "Perhaps it has dried up" added James who knew the climate history. "In the 16th Century we had a major heatwave. It was hot enough to dry up entire lakes so why not a waterfall?" he asked, Ernest nodded in agreement. "Tomorrow we will all go and take a look at this Bedlamite falls" said Ernest rolling up the map and tidying his papers away.

" I sense a storm coming in from the East" he added having a sixth sense for this type of thing his friends new he was right.

As predicted a storm raged over the mountains and glens. The tent was sturdy enough and waterproof. It shook and creaked but was secured to the ground with strong ropes and large pegs driven deep into the soil.

Sleep did not come easy to the group as thoughts of treasures and the storm outside danced around in their minds. Eventually they all dropped off to sleep one by one. When they awoke the rain was still falling. This did not deter them and they all donned sealskin coats and boots before picking up whatever tools and provisions they thought they may need.

As they rounded the top of the hill, Howard spotted a stone Cairn. "Is that a marker or a burial Cairn?" he asked no one particularly. "I would say burial Cairn by the size of it. A well built one too" said James examining the stones. "Should we excavate it?" asked Charles joining James by the pile of rocks. "Yes, as we are here we may as well see what lies beneath" replied James passing the first rock to Charles who placed it feet away.

It took an hour to log and remove each stone. Marking each one individually so they would know where they were originally placed in the pile.

It was a tedious job but they were meticulous and thorough in their work. The remains of Alexander St Clair lay undisturbed for centuries until this day. The man was unrecognisable and his clothes had dissolved so the grave gave no information of use to the group of Archaeologists. After rebuilding the cairn they sat down to rest and enjoy the view around them.

"So, where was this waterfall?" asked Howard through a mouthful of chicken leg. "Somewhere over in that direction" said Ernest pointing Northwards. When they had finished their meal they headed in the direction Ernest had pointed. The heather was soft beneath their feet and it was not until it was almost too late that they came across a large hole in the ground surrounded by bushes and foliage.

"This is it. This is Bedlamite falls!" smiled Ernest. "Come on we must get into this hole and examine it" he added grabbing a rope from his backpack. It was only Six feet to the base but the rope made it easier for the elder of the four men to ascend. On their knees they scraped and dug the ground. Finding sand and pebbles and remains of water dwelling creatures they had the proof this was once a lively river source.

Howard stood up to stretch. He leant against a fragile looking branch behind him and breathed deeply. The Scottish air filled his lungs and he relished the freshness compared to the smog of London. Suddenly the branch broke. He fell backwards through the foliage. "Howard are you alright ?" called James brushing the ferns and branches to one side. Howard lay on his back inside a small cave. "look at this!" he exclaimed excitedly.

"Quick get the lanterns!" shouted James. Ernest and Christopher soon joined them inside the cave. The oil lanterns lit the interior well and the way ahead was visible. Fountains of dust fell from the ceiling as the men made their way through the tunnels and down into the belly of the mountains.

The sight of the treasures in front of the group stopped them in their tracks. Christopher was the first to step toward it. He ran his hands through the piles of gold coins and jewellery. Picking up a ring he slipped it into his pocket without the others noticing.

"This is outstanding" said James finally as they examined the artefacts. "Can this really be?" asked Howard picking up what looked like a small chunk of wood. "If this is what I think it is then we have discovered something beyond all our wildest dreams" he said.

Ernest examined the piece of timber. "I have never seen wood such as this" he said confused. "Perhaps it is part of the true cross" said Howard. "Look here. A Templar sword" he continued pulling the blade from the pile. "If this is part of the true cross then this must be the famed Templar treasure ......" started Ernest.

James stopped him and began reciting a poem.

"In Jesus' time, the dogwood grew To a stately size and a lovely hue.'Twas strong and firm, its branches interwoven. For the cross of Christ its timbers were chosen. Seeing the distress at this use of their wood Christ made a promise which still holds good: "Never again shall the dogwood grow Large enough to be used so. Slender and twisted, it shall be With blossoms like the cross for all to see. As blood stains the petals marked in brown, the blossom's centre wears a thorny crown. All who see it will remember Me crucified on a cross from the dogwood tree. Cherished and protected, this tree shall be a reminder to all of My agony".

Silence was all around them as he finished. Even the air seemed strangely still and unmoving. Suddenly the earth shook beneath their feet and rocks began to fall sending sherds of crystal scattering across the floor and treasure. "We need to get out of here, NOW!" shouted James grabbing Ernest's arm.

Howard and Christopher were already heading toward the exit. The cavern collapsed inwards, showering Ernest and James with debris. Howard and Christopher ran for the surface as the tunnels fell in behind them. A small shaft of light appeared ahead of them. In the darkness Christopher ran and ran. As fast his legs could take him. He jumped the last few feet as the tunnel collapsed killing his father. Christopher struggled to remove the rubble.

For hours he dug and pulled at the rocks. They would not move. And so it was, with a heavy heart, he headed back to the camp site alone.

8 THE EVIL THAT MEN DO

Christopher had returned to London and broken the news of his father, Ernest and James's deaths. He did not speak of the treasure to anyone and continued his life studying medicine.

He forgot about the ring he had picked up in the cave and had thrown it into his medicine bag on his return home. Inside the college a group of men all stood around the room. A table stood central and upon it a man lay.

Christopher steadied his hand and made the incision with his scalpel. Blood seeped from the wound and his colleague mopped it up with a rag. As he reached inside the open wound he removed a black coloured tumour. Wiping the blood away, he took a needle and cotton and sewed the wound up neatly. Removed his gloves and mask then turned and bowed toward a group of men who applauded.

"Congratulations sir, that was an excellent procedure" said one of the men shaking Christopher's hand. Christopher had become a very skilled surgeon over his years of study and this was one of many successful operations he had undertaken.

"Please excuse me while I go clean up and change" he said excusing himself from the entourage of well wishers. He let himself into the communal bathrooms and placed his bag on the wooden bench. Leaving his clothes behind with his bag he slipped into the warm water and lit up a cigar.

Closing his eyes, he never heard the door open. Nor did he hear someone creeping in the shadows. It was not until the door closed behind the criminal as he left that Christopher realised his bag was gone.

White chapel was a rough area full of prostitutes and ruffians. Even the local Bobbies were wary of the streets here. A lone figure walked silently through the streets, a cane in his gloved hands. Darkness is the friend of evil and upon this moonlit night the figure stalked his prey. A young prostitute, Mary-Ann Polly Nicholls, wandered down an alley way to relieve herself.

The figure watched Mary-Ann as she let her panties drop and squatted. Slowly the figure removed his glove, a gold ring adorned his finger. The inscription on the ring that of a Templar cross. He pushed the woman against a wall and with one swift motion slit her throat to the bone.

The streets were dark. Lit only by gas lamps every Twenty yards. Young George cross, a Carter, wandered down Bucks Row pulling his cart of wares ready for the market.

He stopped outside a gate noticing a bundle of rags in the bushes as he bent down to take a closer look another Carter, Robert Paul, arrived. "Ere George what's that then? he asked peering over George's shoulder. "Think it's a dead body Robert, we should go find a Bobby" replied George. The two men sped off down the street. Returning moments later with three Police Constables.

"Okay stand back, let's have a look see!" said PC Neil shining his light on the body. He let the beam of his torch wander over her once pretty face then to her neck with the clear slice. It was then he noticed something else. Something so gruesome it would haunt the five men for the rest of their lives.

A large gash ran down Mary-Anne's abdomen. Her organs removed with precision. The sight was too much for all of them and between bouts of vomiting PC Neil blew on his whistle to alert all officers to the scene of the crime.

In a dark room in the halls of the Royal College of Surgeons a figure cleaned his surgical tools with a rag and chemicals. He placed them one by one in the bag by his side. Twisting the gold ring he wore on his finger he removed it and placed it on the table before climbing into bed. His dreams would be haunted with guilt for killing Mary-Anne Polly Nicholls that night.

Inspector Frederick Avaline examined the victim. In the daylight it was much easier to see the mutilation the killer had left behind and though it turned his stomach he did his job as a professional would.

"It appears we have a man who understands medicine on our hands" he said to the constable who stood beside him trying not to look at the corpse. "Are you okay constable? You look a bit Err, green around the gills" he drew his finger around his own face.

The policeman grimaced, turned, and removing his helmet vomited into it. "It's okay constable we don't all have the stomach for this" said Frederick patting the policeman on the back which immediately made him remove the contents of his stomach once more.

Back in his office at Scotland Yard, Inspector Avaline sat at His desk twirling a pen between his fingers in thought. This was one of the most brutal killings he had come across in his whole career on the force and he was determined to find the culprit.

Through out the next Three months there were Four more murders in White chapel. Each victim was said to be of ill repute. Each victim was a woman. And in every case, the body had been left mutilated. The incisions of the wounds made by the sharpest of blades.

The cold November rain fell as a figure boarded a ship bound for Australia. Among his luggage, a bag of surgical tools.

"Good day Doctor, I hope you enjoy your journey" said the Captain of the vessel as he greeted the man.

In the dark room of the royal college of surgeons. The gold ring lay on the table. Forgotten? Perhaps.

Maybe left behind for the evil it made the man do.

No one knew why it had been left behind or where it disappeared to.

Epilogue:

The evil of man is not in some trinket of gold or ancient artefact once cursed by a dying man. Evil is buried deep within a person's soul and all it takes to bring that darkness out could be an act of jealousy, greed or lust.   This is not to say all men and women are evil or have this devil inside them. For some it is easier to forgive. To forget and to love.

But they do it not in the name of a higher being or treasures to line their pockets. They love because they can. They love because it is the honest way.

They love because others do not. They love, simply because it is human to do so.

ABOUT THE AUTHOR

Phillip Ross is a West Yorkshire based Author, Artist, Photographer and Musician.

The Templar Curse is Phillip's Second book to be released

Other Titles by Phillip Ross:

The Quest Volume One

Printed in Great Britain
by Amazon.co.uk, Ltd.,
Marston Gate.